D1452919

THE WOMAN WHO BUILT A BRIDGE

Center Point
Large Print

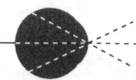

**This Large Print Book carries the
Seal of Approval of N.A.V.H.**

THE WOMAN WHO BUILT A BRIDGE

C. K. CRIGGER

CENTER POINT LARGE PRINT
THORNDIKE, MAINE

This Center Point Large Print edition
is published in the year 2022 by arrangement with
Wolfpack Publishing.

The text of this Large Print edition is unabridged.
In other aspects, this book may vary
from the original edition.
Printed in the United States of America
on permanent paper sourced using
environmentally responsible foresting methods.
Set in 16-point Times New Roman type.

ISBN: 978-1-63808-493-8

The Library of Congress has cataloged this record
under Library of Congress Control Number: 2022940826

CHAPTER 1

Shay Billings rode Hoot, his gray gelding, past the old Schutt place twice in the space of a week before it registered. "It" being the scent of woodsmoke the first time, and the crow of a chicken the second. 'Course, between being on the opposite side of the stream and taking the time to wend his way a couple extra miles to the closest ford, he didn't figure it was worth his time to investigate. Schutt's derelict barn didn't seem to be on fire and, anyway, it wasn't any of his business.

Wrapped up in his own concerns over the last couple months, like seeing all his calves and foals safely delivered, and paying for the seed oats and alfalfa for the two fields he'd about killed himself getting ready to plant, he was too tired to care about anything else. Not even the rumors going around about Marvin Hammel building a sawmill and damming the river to harness the power. T. T. Thurston, owner of the mercantile, had told him Hammel wasn't being too careful whose toes he stepped on either. Or, more accurately, whose water downstream got diminished. Shay was just glad to be upstream and on a tributary instead of the river.

But the third time he passed ten days later, when he saw the patch of spaded ground out behind the

5

old barn, well, that did draw his attention. Even so, it wasn't the most important thing. No, siree! The important thing plumb made his eyes bug out.

"Whoa, Hoot," he said, upon which Hoot whoa'd. Shay was a soft-spoken, patient trainer of animals who liked teaching verbal commands. Folding his hands over the saddle horn, he studied the place. "What do you make of that?" he asked the horse.

Hoot shook his head, bridle and bit rattling.

"Yeah. Me neither."

In the interval between his last trip to town and this one, somebody had been mighty busy. The old Kindred Crossing bridge, abandoned these many years and deemed too dangerous for a man walking let alone for critters or vehicles to traverse, sported new joists, braces, and planks. The freshly-milled wood shone a bright rosy gold color, resin still rising in amber beads under the hot spring sun.

"Well, Hoot," Shay said, "let's you and me give'er a try." He clucked to the horse who turned from the longer road toward the bridge. A sign had been nailed to the anchor post.

Toll Bridge
5¢—Pay On Other Side

A nickel, he thought. And worth it. Especially now with the river still high down at the ford.

Last time he'd been this way there'd been a drowned calf tossed up on the riverbank. Not one of his, for which he was grateful.

Apparently, there was no attendant waiting to collect the fee; only a tin can with a slot in the lid affixed to the handrail on the other side.

"A trusting soul," Shay murmured, which caused Hoot to bob his head in agreement. "Reckon we should stop by and say howdy when we come back from town?" He fished a nickel out of his pocket, dropped it through the slot and rode on, fully intending to make the bridge keeper's acquaintance on his way home.

As it happened, he didn't, having instead stopped at Bud Knowles's Barefoot Saloon, the local watering hole, for a well-deserved shot or two of good sipping whiskey after concluding his business.

Turned out some of his neighbors were there before him. They'd claimed a table and were involved in a desultory game of five-card stud, betting pennies on the outcome. Nobody had the cash money to risk hard-earned dollars.

Bent Langley saw him first and waved him over to the card-players' table. "Take a pew, Billings. I ain't seen you since the Thanksgiving dance and them women were hangin' all over you. How's it going over to your place? Stock come through the winter all right?"

Shay felt his face heating up like a pot-bellied

stove. Leave it to Bent to bring up the Inman sisters. Dang it! It wasn't like he could push them off with a broom handle. Should've known he'd come in for a ribbing.

Pulling out a chair, he sat. Over at the bar, Bud Knowles, proprietor and bartender, pointed to a dusty bottle and held up two fingers. Shay nodded and pointed around to the others, indicating a refill. He spun a dollar onto the table when Bud brought his drink.

Bent, fortunately for Shay's equanimity, dropped the subject of females soon enough and brought up a more serious topic. In fact, it was Shay's closest neighbor who was the center of attention. Apparently, this get-together was in the way of a farewell send-off. Jim Scott had sold out and was moving farther north, up toward Metaline.

"Where the land is cheaper," he said.

"Yeah," Bent Langley agreed. "But the soil is thinner and spring is a long time comin'. You're as much a farmer as you are a rancher, Jim. This is better farming country. You should stay."

"Better ranching country hereabouts, too," Shay added, frowning at Jim. "What does your wife have to say about moving?"

Jim fumbled with his cards. He was down to four pennies on the table in front of him. "She don't like leaving. The school here . . ." He faltered and looked away.

Bent and Bo Cobb exchanged a glance.

"It's a good school," Shay said. He should know, seeing he'd been instrumental in working with John Rankin Rogers, back before John became governor, to make it more than a one-room, one-teacher educational stop-gap. Back then, it'd been only a little better than nothing. And as he remembered, Miz Scott had been one who'd been real happy when her youngest went off to school.

"I know." Jim swallowed the last inch of beer in his mug and stood up. "Speaking of the wife, I'd better get home. Got a lot to do by the end of the week."

"Who'd you sell to, Jim?" Shay's question dropped into the conversation like a boatload of ballast.

Jim's mouth opened, then closed. After a time, he said, "Reckon I'd better not answer that, boys. Sorry."

The three men at the table stared at each other when Jim had gone.

"What the hell?" Bo looked dumbfounded.

Bent's fingers were drumming on the table. "Something is going on. Something shady. Jim just ups and leaves after all his hard work? It don't make sense."

"I'll be sorry to see the last of him and his family." Shay had the deal. He spun cards out to Bent and Cobb. "They've been good neighbors."

Bo Cobb shoved his last penny into the pot. "As I remember, they kept an eye on your place when you was gone working for the governor last winter."

Shay nodded. He'd been grateful, especially since the place had been in apple-pie order when he got home. Including every one of his prized Langshan hens.

Cobb studied his hand before folding and tossing his cards onto the table. "Gotta say I agree with Bent. Something shady is going on. Why else ain't Jim talking?"

Frowning down at his cards, Bent cocked his head. "He said one thing before you got here, Shay. But it didn't make much sense."

"What was it?" Shay asked.

"Said his well would soon be dry. I says to him, 'What the hell you talkin' about? River's higher than anytime these last five years.' A funny look passed over his face and he shrugged. Wouldn't say anything else."

They could've talked all afternoon and never come up with an answer.

Shay's indulgence with bourbon and cards made him a little late getting home for chores, even though he took the short way and was mighty grateful for the new bridge. A nickel seemed a bargain to avoid the extra miles.

And then he forgot all about the smoke and the crowing chicken and the garden spot and, yes, even the bridge itself in the rush of finishing his spring work. Well, that and the way the Scott family moved out practically overnight. The incident had Shay more worried than any strange goings-on around Schutt's old barn, that's for dang sure.

One of Cobb's hands, seeing Shay in the far meadow helping a heifer birth her first calf, had the latest scuttlebutt. Seemed Bent Langley and Marvin Hammel had gotten into it over who owned the water flowing downriver toward the Columbia. Bent lived downstream at the falls, beyond both the Scott place and Hammel's. The story was that Hammel had blocked off a portion of the river where it passed through his land which slowed Bent's water to a trickle. Left enough to provide for the house and Pinky Langley's kitchen garden but not enough to water his orchard or irrigate the field where he had a hundred head of prime Hereford breeding stock growing fat. If he didn't get water, they wouldn't be fat long, everybody knew that.

And here opinions diverged. Some folks grew heated. One set of folks figured Hammel could do whatever he wanted with the water that ran through his property. Another set figured the river's flow was a natural resource that pretty much belonged to everybody and no single somebody had the right to deny his neighbors the use of it. Surely there was enough for everybody, long as one person didn't hog it.

As for Shay, well, he was just glad his spread lay above the kerfuffle, closer to the mountains on his own year-round creek where he didn't have to worry about one of his neighbors poaching water. So far, anyhow, though come to think on it even his stream ran into the larger one. But in his own mind, he sided with Bent. This wasn't the desert where every drop was a precious commodity. But then they didn't live in a rain forest either. Fair, he figured, was fair.

The biggest puzzle to Shay's mind was why Hammel figured he needed every drop of that water so badly he'd deliberately deprive his neighbors of it. And while he was at it cause a whole lot of hard feelings. Dangerous feelings. A dam big enough to generate power for a sawmill shouldn't require the whole river.

Just as well for him, Shay figured, if he stayed close to home and kept his nose clean.

Brin, which was short for Brindle and admittedly not a real creative kind of name for a brindle-colored hound dog, set to yodeling a cry that could turn from welcoming to warning in an instant.

Shay looked up from the disagreeable job of digging a new pit to go under his outhouse, glad for any sort of interruption. A feller riding a big brown horse had broken from the band of trees down by the stream that rushed across his property, watering a towering grove of poplars along the way. The horse ambled, taking its time as it pushed through a half-dozen of Shay's beeves toward the house. The meadow grass they grazed on was a healthy dark green, thick and lush.

"Hush, Brin," Shay said. "It's just Bent Langley. No cause for a fuss." He hoped, anyhow, remembering the gossip he'd heard in town.

Langley's brown horse was easily recognizable from the distance, being larger than the average saddle pony. Langley, himself, was larger than the average-sized rancher which made the pair of them memorable. They were accompanied by one of Langley's sons, the middle one Shay thought, although he disremembered young Langley's proper handle.

Shay went on digging, watching the riders from under the brim of his hat. This being one of those jobs a feller doesn't want to brag about, he felt a little embarrassed getting caught at it. Then he laughed at himself. Wasn't a place in the whole world didn't have the same problem to contend with and at least his sewie-hole was a safe distance from the source of his drinking water, unlike some others he could name.

After a bit, the riders pulled alongside him and stopped, the horse blowing a spray of snot toward the dog.

Brin growled but not as if her heart was in it.

"Howdy, Billings," Langley said, studying the growing pit. "Helluva job you got going for yourself. Hot today, too."

Shay stabbed his shovel into the pile of loose dirt where it stood quivering. Taking off his hat, he wiped sweat from his eyes. Shirtless, his shoulders, still winter-white in the spring weather, had taken on a pink glow.

"That it is, Bent. Hot, I mean." He nodded toward the pair. "Light a spell and rest your backsides." He reached for the canteen he'd left sitting under the blackberry bushes he'd found growing here when he first arrived. Had no idea where they'd sprung from, but the bushes had good berries in season if a man wanted to risk life and limb amongst the thorns to get at them. They threw a thick shade that kept the canteen fairly cool. He offered Bent the container. "Water?"

"Don't mind if I do." Langley dismounted and took the canteen, drinking deep and splashing some of the water over his face and letting the residue trickle down his neck. "Good," he said, handing it on to his son. He gazed out over the green meadow and some of the fat beeves to where the creek ran. "And plenty of it."

Shay stirred uneasily. "What brings you out this way, if you don't mind me asking? Not that I don't welcome the company but I'd've figured you'd be hard at work branding those new calves of yours."

"Me and the boys got'er done. Now I'm lookin' for a stray cow. Or a rustled one." The toe of Bent's boot worked a circle in the dirt Shay'd dug out of the pit. The boy shifted restlessly as though wanting to get a move on.

Looking hard at his neighbor, Shay's eyes narrowed. "This is some piece for a cow to stray."

Bent looked off into the distance. "It is, ain't it? But it's part and parcel of what has been going on downstream from here."

Shay opened his mouth to contest the downstream part but he reminded himself that technically, although Bent meant the main river, his creek still ran into it.

"Rustlers?" He looked out over his own small herd. "They ain't come this far, not that I'm complaining." He touched the hound's head. "Ole Brin is getting lazy with nothing to do."

"You better be glad you've been left in peace." Bent didn't look happy. "So far. But rustlers ain't even the worst of it. It's the water being stole. You hear about Hammel?"

Shay figured he would've had to move a thousand miles east not to have. "Heard more rumors," he admitted, "when I met up with Bo Cobb the other day. Don't know if I can believe all I was told."

"You can if somebody said Hammel has cut

a channel and dammed off most of the river at his home place. Believe it. He ain't hardly left enough water running to take a bath in at the old Scott place or mine, let alone Richardson who lives farther down. His livestock is hurting and Dave's had to dig a well halfway to Chiner to get enough for the house."

"Why?"

"Why what?"

"Why has Hammel dammed off the water?" This was the part Shay couldn't figure.

Bent gawked at him with a surprised look on his weathered face. "Didn't Bo tell you that part? Marvin Hammel says he's putting in a sawmill, that's why, complete with electricity powered by the falls and his own turbine. He plans to sell the extra electricity and get rich. Richer. So he's building a big ole mill pond to make sure he ain't the one who runs out of water. Got a regular lake fillin' up in the gully behind his mill."

He spat into the hole Shay was digging; his boy, who had yet to say a word, copying. "Says he's just puttin' the land back the way the good Lord made it but, hell, that gully ain't held water since the ice age a thousand years ago." His forehead twisted in thought. "Ten thousand, maybe."

Shay lifted his hat and scratched his head. "You mention this water grabbing business to Sheriff Rhodes, Bent?"

Langley's face swelled up until it looked like

16

a turkey gobbler's neck and turned just as red.

"I talked to him," he replied grimly. "Tried to. He just stared over my shoulder and told me there ain't anything he can do. Said Hammel had a right to manage his own property. Said maybe I should sell out to Hammel. Me and Richardson both. And by damn, it wasn't twenty-four hours before Hammel shows up and makes me an offer. A low-ball offer."

At his side, the boy was nodding although Shay couldn't decide whether the nod meant he agreed with the sheriff or that he'd witnessed the exchange and was verifying his father's words.

"He said," Langley continued, "Richardson was talking to Hammel's lawyer and maybe I should get in on the deal before the price went down. Hell, nobody'd sell for what he offered in the first place."

Shay spent a moment studying a few white clouds floating in the sky overhead before opening his mouth. He didn't want mixed in the middle of his neighbors' fight as he had a notion Hammel would make a bad enemy but, hell, this just didn't sound right. First Jim Scott and now Langley and the Richardson outfit?

"Better get your own lawyer, Bent," he said. "And make sure whose side he's working on."

Bent's face drooped although his son's took on a fierce look.

"That's what I figured you'd say," Bent said, kind of dispirited-like.

The advice seemed to resound with Bent's son. "Too late for that." His voice crackled with what might've been excitement. "We'd better get ready to fight."

About then, Brin rose up from where she'd been laying in shade cast by the blackberry bushes and nosed Shay's hand. He fondled her long ears, hoping the familiar motion might ease the unsettled feeling Langley's visit had wrought.

"You'd better hope it don't come to that," he said.

The next day, another visitor interrupted Shay as he labored at setting a few new posts in his fence line. He couldn't say as he particularly welcomed the man who rode up on a jaded horse. The horse frothed white foam around the bit. Shay found it necessary to bite his tongue to keep from speaking up. He had no respect for a man who mistreated his animals.

But he sure as hell was curious.

Two visitors in two days. The occurrence set some kind of new record, seeing as how weeks were likely to pass without his talking to another soul. Especially in the spring when everyone was working themselves to the bone. Except this one, apparently. For one thing, he was dressed too fine. Shined boots, creased trousers even aboard a horse, starched white shirt turned a little gray from the dust churned up on the road.

Brin roused herself out of the shade of the work wagon and bayed a greeting.

"To what do I owe the honor?" Shay paused his work and leaned on his posthole diggers. Sweat poured off him, his breath came short. Exchanging the diggers for his canteen where it lay in the meager shade of a rock outcropping, he took a couple quick swigs before, mindful of his manners, he offered it to Marvin Hammel. "Hush, Brin," he told the hound.

Hammel shook his head. He had a canteen of his own hanging from his saddle horn. Wrapped in a wooly material that held moisture, it'd been soaked in a bucket of water before he rode out. From the look of things, the fabric had begun to dry which meant warm water in the canteen.

To tell the truth, Shay's feelings weren't in the least hurt by the man's refusal of his hospitality. Had to laugh at himself, though, when he found himself grateful Hammel hadn't caught him digging the new privy hole.

"Whose side are you on?" Hammel demanded. A scowl contorted a face that might've been called handsome if his mouth, under a thin mustache, hadn't been set in such stubborn and petulant lines.

"Side?" Pulling his bandana from a back pocket, Shay mopped his forehead.

"Mine or Langley's? Whose side?"

Well, Shay thought, that was something Hammel had no right asking. Time he dug in his heels. "Don't know what you're talking about." He took another sip of water, poured some into his hat and offered it to Brin who lapped up every drop.

"The stupid act don't become you," Hammel said, his washed-denim blue eyes scanning Shay's meadowland as though taking stock. "I know Langley stopped here yesterday."

Just how, Shay wondered, did Hammel know that? And what did he mean, "stupid"?

"Do you?" Shay rolled his shoulders in a carefree shrug. "Ain't against the law for a neighborly visit, last I heard." He met Hammel's squinty eyes. "Just like this one right now. It is neighborly, ain't it?"

Tucking the canteen back under the outcropping, he picked up the posthole diggers and plunged them into the ground. Maybe they went down a little deeper than usual, fueled by a surge of anger he took care not to show on his face.

He didn't know what bee Hammel had boring a new hole in his ass but he didn't like it.

Hammel's horse swung its hindquarters around, hooves dangerously close to the newly opened hole in the ground. Shay jumped aside, batting the horse's rump to put some distance between them. Hammel feigned not to notice.

"What did you talk about?" Hammel sawed on the reins, the horse's mouth opening under the rough treatment.

Bastard. Shay's eyes narrowed. "I don't know as it's any of your business what we talked about. That's between him and me."

Hammel's lips lifted in a snarl. "I figure I know without you saying but here's a word of advice. Take care what side you're on, Billings. You don't want to back the losing horse. When there's money concerned, whoever has the most wins. And I've got the most."

Coolly, or at least he hoped he appeared cool even though his face felt hot, Shay forced a slight smile. "Who you threatening, Hammel? Me or Langley? See, I don't have a horse in this race but I don't mind watching all the runners keep to fair play."

"No horse? That's where you're mistaken, Billings. You live here, you've gotta have a horse."

With that, digging in his spurs, Hammel put his horse into a lope, clouds of dust rising from the little-used road.

Overhead, a red-tailed hawk screeched in victory as it came out of a dive holding some small critter, mouse or rabbit, in its beak. A predator, same as the man who'd just ridden away.

He'd had to have the last word, too. The worst part was Shay figured Hammel could be right.

Living here, it'd be hard to stay out of any quarrels between neighbors and it looked like this particular quarrel could turn into a war.

Worrying didn't mend his fence. Shay thrust the diggers in the hole, elbows jarred as he struck a rock.

Shay had his third visitor, fourth if you took Bent Langley's son into consideration, a day and a half after Marvin Hammel's unsettling interruption of his fence building. This time, he was in the barn spreading fresh bedding in a stall where a mare had needed help as she foaled later in the spring than Shay liked.

Brin warned of the rider as soon as the bay horse turned off the main road and headed toward the buildings.

Shay walked out into the sunlight, still carrying the pitchfork.

"I see him," he told Brin who quieted right down. He straightened his back, stretching out an ache between his shoulders that had come on after the fence-building exercise.

When still some distance off, the rider removed his hat and waved it over his head. A friendly sign Shay considered good.

Turned out it wasn't. Oh, the feller was friendly enough. The message he brought, the opposite.

Shay recognized him from last fall when ranchers' roundabouts scoured the countryside for strays. When they'd been gathered up, they were separated out according to brand and driven to their home range.

The hand, fresh-faced with youth, drew his horse to a stop right in front of Shay. "Howdy, Mr. Billings," he said, the title making Shay feel older than his twenty-eight years. "Bo sent me. I got some news he figured you ought to hear about."

Turns out he worked for Bo Cobb whose spread lay about six miles south of Shay's.

"Good news or bad?" Shay asked.

"Bad." The hand's face drooped sorrowfully.

"Then I don't want to hear it." Even so, Shay knew there was no way to avoid listening to what the lad had to say. And he was right. The hand whose name Shay finally remembered was John Johnson, memorable only because it wasn't, took his words as an invitation and started right in relating his tale.

"It's Bent Langley's boy." Johnson's blue eyes flashed. He seemed a little excited by the drama as he announced, "He's been shot. Bushwhacked."

A sick feeling curled around Shay's guts. "Shot dead?"

"Yep. His brother said his horse ran into the yard with the stirrups flapping so he went looking for him. Found him lying in the trail a half-mile from home."

"Murdered."

"Yep."

"Which of Bent's boys was it?" The firebrand? Shay wondered. The boy who'd been ready to take on a fight?

Johnson shrugged. "Dunno. Only fifteen, though. Bo didn't say a name. Said to tell you the funeral will be tomorrow at the cemetery outside town. Gonna be a little meeting after." He paused. "Hammel nor the sheriff are invited." Mission completed, he reined his horse to head back the way he'd come.

"You tell the feller down there at the bridge about the funeral?" Shay called after him.

The lad turned in his saddle and shook his head. "Nope. Didn't see nobody around to talk to or I would've. The bridge sure is fine though. Saved me a good two hours getting here and back."

Shay nodded. "It did that."

An inclination to mosey over and see if he could talk to whoever'd repaired the bridge hit as Shay drank a cup of reheated coffee and chewed a slab of cold beef at noon. So far, nobody appeared to have seen or talked to the mysterious source of the good deed.

The few who lived or had business on this side of the river had cause to be grateful to that benefactor, even at a nickel per crossing. But what if that wasn't the point? What if this was only a way to lay claim to the land, the old abandoned homestead with its falling-down barn and, most importantly, the ford on the river?

What if this was more of Hammel's doing?

Seemed to him he'd better find out before the meeting tomorrow.

CHAPTER 2

January Schutt watched through gaps in the boards still clinging to the barn's frame as the young rider returned from wherever he'd been and crossed the river. He stopped at the can nailed to the bridge post and dropped something in the slot. Supposed to be a nickel and usually a nickel is what she found. Or five pennies sometimes. Or sometimes nothing at all. Some folks just liked to see what they could get away with. So far none of the rare travelers had taken the can.

She watched the man gawk around, too. Hoping to catch sight of her, no doubt. Or someone anyway. He didn't know it was her exactly. Just whoever'd fixed the bridge. Which, she was bound to say, hadn't been the easiest task she'd ever undertaken.

But not the hardest either.

No. That honor belonged to her being here at all. Here at the old Schutt homestead, she meant. And alive, despite her grandfather's best efforts all those years ago.

When the rider disappeared over the hill toward town, January took her hand from Penelope—Pen for short—her big black dog. Pen had curly hair and weighed maybe seventy pounds. January had no idea what sort of breeding the dog had sprung

26

from. She only knew Pen was a good companion and her best friend.

Her only friend. And smart, too.

But Pen, being a curious soul, would've liked to greet the rider while January wanted no part of socializing. Her rare trips to town, five in the almost five months she'd been back, had been painful enough. If she hadn't had a surplus of butter and eggs to sell, she probably wouldn't have made half of the five.

Pen and January emerged from the dark area of the barn where she'd put up a wall, deceptive in that a casual glance didn't show a wall at all but only a continuation of a falling-down stall.

Paint and clever construction had worked well for her so far. At least, as long as no intruder got far enough inside the barn to make a close examination of the area. She intended to see they didn't. If they tried, she had a couple little surprises for them, sure to discourage further inroads into her domain.

"C'mon, Pen," she said. "Time to get to work. I want to get my beans and corn in the ground today."

Huffing a little, Pen trotted along beside her while January, back in the garden behind the barn, dragged her hoe through the soil to make rows. The dog lost interest, though, when it came time to drop seeds into the shallow trench. She went to lie in the shade.

January, hot, tired and sweaty, soon became immersed in the rhythm of her work. Her hoe scritched in the dirt. Doves called from the cottonwood grove overlooking the river. The stream, still running high with snow melt rushing down from the mountains, chuckled as it passed over boulders left behind when the glaciers formed the river bed.

Working hard at the repetitious chore, January eventually became almost as sleepy as Pen.

Until a quiet "Howdy" from behind startled her and she froze, her hoe lifted in mid-stroke.

If it hadn't been for the fact the figure was wearing a sunbonnet, Shay'd have thought a slim boy stood before him. Finally, though, he decided it was a woman wearing men's clothes. First time he'd seen a woman wearing trousers. Not that he minded but they did show a little more of her anatomy than he was used to seeing right out in public.

More of her bottom half, anyway. A loose, billowing shirt covered up most everything on top which he figured might be too bad. And the bonnet had such a wide brim he had no idea what kind of face was concealed beneath it. A thick mahogany-colored braid of hair hung down her back. He thought she must be young, going by the easy way she moved.

Except, right at this moment, she stood still as

a stone idol or like a deer transfixed by a bright light.

"Howdy, ma'am," he said again as if he took no notice of her odd choice of attire. Or her even odder reception of his presence.

Slowly, she turned sideways to him. Her head dipped. "Looks like I need to put up 'No Trespassing' signs," she said, seemingly to no one.

Shay decided he was a little offended by that. It wasn't like he'd done or said a thing to warrant her dislike, let alone her downright unfriendly words. But he was here and he figured it'd be best to hurry up and have his say, then leave.

"Sorry to bother you." Thoroughly uncomfortable, he twitched the reins. Hoot sidled, a front hoof coming near the edge of her garden. "Just trying to be neighborly. Name of Shay Billings. My spread is closest to you, up on Rock Creek a few miles."

"Mr. Billings." She nodded slight acknowledgement. "What do you want?"

"I don't want anything, ma'am. This here bridge is your doing, ain't it?"

"It is. If you have a problem with the toll, go on down to the ford. I'm not forcing you to cross the stream here."

Shay took a breath. Prickly, by gum. "No problem, ma'am. Purely opposite. I wanted to

29

thank you. The bridge is real handy to folks. Saves us some time."

"Glad you approve."

Huh. Could've fooled him. He took another of those breaths. "Next thing is, there's been a killing hereabouts and I thought, in case you hadn't heard already, you oughta know about it."

She shifted toward him, then away again. "A killing? Do you mean a murder?"

"Yes, ma'am, I do." At least she appeared in favor of plain speaking which suited him fine.

"Who was the victim?"

Before he could answer, she let out an eardrum-piercing whistle that nearly deafened him. A few seconds later, a beastie came running out of the cottonwoods toward them. A dog, its tongue lolling in apparent joy at having company, stopped to touch noses with Hoot.

"Pen," the woman said, a reprimand. Her voice, though soft and low, was a little gravelly as though not often used. The dog's ears drooped as it instantly twirled and sat at the woman's side, stiff and alert like a soldier at parade rest.

Shay smiled at the sight.

"Who was murdered?" she asked again, seeming more comfortable with the dog beside her.

"A family by the name of Langley lives a few miles southwest of here, on the river. One of their boys. Fifteen years old, is all. Shot dead when he was only a half-mile from home."

"Why?"

"Why? Don't know, ma'am. Not for sure. Likely a warning of some kind. The boy's funeral is tomorrow. Gonna be a meeting afterward. Maybe we'll find out then but there's been talk of a feller hogging more water from the river than he ought. He cut off the flow downriver and tried to buy Bent Langley out for a little of nothing. Got Langley's back up. Could be about that. There's hard feelings all around. Drove off one family already, I hear."

"Classic," she said which he thought was kind of a strange thing to say.

"Classic, ma'am?"

"Land or water. Water or land. The same old reasons for men to fight. Next thing you know, it'll be over air."

"Yes, ma'am. I reckon it will." Even so, he looked out into the distance thinking all the wide-open space made that unlikely.

She had nothing more to say, merely looking at him from under her sunbonnet's wide brim. At least he guessed she was. He couldn't tell a thing about her expression, what with her face held in deep shadow.

"Well," he said at last, "I just thought you ought to know the situation in case that boy of Bo Cobb's neglected to stop by with the message about the murder. Or in case you wanted to attend

31

the funeral." With the response, or lack thereof, he'd gotten from her, he didn't figure it probable.

But then maybe she just plain didn't like his looks. Couldn't blame her any. No doubt he appeared a bit scruffy considering he'd been working hard the morning long. Might stink a bit, too.

If so, she didn't let on.

"Thank you, Mr. Billings, for the information."

He nodded. "Let's go, Hoot," he said, upon which Hoot, with no direction other than those three words, scooted around and started off the way they'd come. She—it struck Shay she hadn't told him her name—must've released the dog because, like a black streak, the creature ran alongside Hoot until they reached the bridge.

The dog stopped there. Shay didn't. Not even long enough to drop a nickel in her can. In all fairness, he didn't figure a neighborly visit called for a toll.

Hoot's hooves sounded hollow on the bridge. The dog sat down in the middle of the road and watched them cross, looking forlorn.

January, once certain Billings had gone, went back to her gardening, covering the rows of beans and the hills of corn with their careful three seeds per mound. The peace hard work usually gave her had fled. Although she berated herself for it, she lost the natural rhythm of planting, the smooth and tamp, smooth and tamp.

She put part of the blame on Pen. Why hadn't the dog warned her of Billings's approach? But then she remembered the dog, who'd been her constant companion for more than ten years, was old. Slowing down, not as alert or fierce as when she'd been young. When they'd both been young. Her dad had brought the pup home on the occasion of January's thirteenth birthday.

Her gaze drifted to the knoll above the barn before, stubbornly, it flicked away again. No point in remembering what lie up there. Think of Pen who'd come to her soon after. Pen, her only friend. Her only comfort. The only one to ever see her as she was. As who she was.

What, the errant thought came to her with the strokes of her hoe, did this Shay Billings think of her about now? She could guess.

"You liked him, didn't you, Pen?"

At the sound of her name, the dog leaned against January's leg.

"And his horse, too. Hoot. He called it Hoot. A funny name for a horse, isn't it? I wonder how he came up with it? Do you suppose he heard an owl just when he was deciding on a name?"

Pen chuffed deep in her throat.

Billings would be thinking her cold and unfriendly. Ungrateful, too, as it had been neighborly of him to come tell her about the murder and to thank her for the work on the bridge. She

33

bet he'd have liked to ask her how she'd done it, a woman alone. Where had she learned the skills necessary? Had she had help?

A funny feeling rose up inside. One that said she wished she could have talked with him about those skills. About her teacher. Even about the recent murder. An urge to talk out loud to someone other than Pen almost overwhelmed her. She longed to go out to where her horse and her mule and the cow were pastured, catch up the horse and ride off in the direction Shay Billings had pointed when he said he lived a few miles away.

Maybe he had a wife. Someone to talk to about women things. Someone who'd help fill the vast emptiness within her.

She wouldn't do it though.

As quickly as the urge came, she quelled it, sending it deep down inside to hide. Better to be lonely than an object of rude curiosity. Or worse yet, of disgust.

The hoe dug too deeply for a few yards. Until she realized and had to go back, carefully pulling off a couple inches of soil. The beans would never come up buried so far down.

"Hah! Better if it's just you and me, Pen. I can tell you any secret and know it's safe." January straightened and cast a wary glance around.

Nothing. They were alone.

Dusk was advancing when January finished the

planting, cleaned her tools like Dad had taught her, and put them away. Whistling Pen to her, they walked the path they'd worn through the grass to the pasture and called in the critters for the night. The cow needed milked.

CHAPTER 3

Shay grinned as Hoot trotted across the bridge the next morning. This being their fifth trip back and forth, the horse acted like he'd been doing it all his life. Their first time across, the hollow feel beneath his hooves had made him a tad nervous, complete with some head-tossing and prancing like an A-rab instead of the fine stock horse he was.

After crossing, they stopped by the post with the can nailed to it and Shay dropped in five of the pennies he'd won off Bent and Bo Cobb at the poker game a while back. It gave him a chance to gaze around as he pretended to count out the money. Didn't see hide nor hair of her though. "Her" being the woman who lived in the barn. Or he supposed she did. As far as he knew, no other building even halfway usable was left on the previously-abandoned homestead and he didn't suppose she'd want to take up residence in the chicken coop. Still, how anyone could live in as rundown a structure as the barn was a puzzle to him. He'd rather endure a snowstorm in a tent than contend with years-old moldy hay, rotten wood, spiders and mice. And maybe skunks, too, he added to the list of undesirables as he sniffed the air.

"C'mon, Hoot," he muttered. "We ain't got all day if we want to make the service."

He guessed correctly, as it happened, she wouldn't be attending the Langley boy's funeral. He'd just as soon not either. A man couldn't ignore a funeral though. Not and remain a good neighbor.

Once past the bridge, the road spiraled out ahead of him. The countryside, lush with the greenest grass of the year, spread open on either side of the river which ran through the center of the valley. Cattle, white-faced Herefords for the most part, stood up to their knees, grazing to their hearts' content. Fields planted in wheat bore sprouts several inches high.

Shay rested his eyes on the scene, drowsing some in the heat. The late May day sported June temperatures and Shay had been going short of sleep, trying to get all his field work done while the weather held.

There'd been previous times he'd napped and let Hoot find his own way between home and town. Today wasn't one of those times. The Langley boy had been ambushed and shot somewhere along this road and Shay had no intention of becoming a second victim. Not that anybody had cause to shoot him.

Turns out it wasn't gunmen he had to worry about. Not that the Inman women weren't every bit as dangerous.

He caught up with them a mile outside of town as they tooled along in their little red-painted buggy being drawn by a fine Morgan gelding. They lived well away from the river, far enough he supposed to be out of the line of contention when it came to using the water. Which didn't mean they weren't able and ready to voice an opinion on the subject.

"Yoohoo, Mr. Billings! Well met," one of the women called to him, waving as if he might not see her unless she drew notice to herself. The other woman kept her attention on driving the horse. The Morgan was a good buggy horse, his pace quick and steady.

The Inman women were twins. Shay never could remember which was Rebecca and which was Ruth. He blamed himself for the memory lapse since they weren't anything alike in looks or in name. Neither one was exactly a beauty either which may have accounted for the fact they were unmarried at the ripe old age of what he estimated at thirty. Neither had given up on finding a husband, the reason Shay found them worrisome. He was well aware one or the other— or both—had him in her sights.

Hoot soon caught up to them.

"Ladies." Shay tipped his hat and clucked a little to Hoot as they drew even, urging him to passing speed.

"Oh, Mr. Billings," the one driving cooed as

she pulled into his way before he could get past, "are you on the way to Joseph Langley's funeral? We are, too. We might as well travel along together."

Doubting any graceful way to decline the invitation existed, Shay resigned himself to playing escort the last mile. "Sad doings, ain't it?"

At least he knew the boy's name now and could give proper condolences without embarrassing himself or distressing Bent or Pinky.

"It is," the one with drab blonde hair said. "We heard Sheriff Rhodes came out and looked around where Arthur found his brother's body but he didn't discover any clues. Sheriff Rhodes, I mean, didn't discover any clues."

"No surprise there." The brown-haired one, tart as a raw gooseberry, slapped the lines on the horse's back in emphasis.

Shay was inclined to agree. Rhodes was a lazy bugger, for sure.

"Oh, don't be so hard on him, Ruth," the blonde said. "I believe he does his best."

"Best for himself," Brown replied. "And maybe what's best for Marvin Hammel."

Brown equals Ruth. Blonde equals Rebecca. Shay tried to commit the information to memory. So just what did Ruth mean when she said, "Best for Marvin Hammel?"

"What do you think, Mr. Billings?" She, Ruth

39

that is, asked Shay directly over her sister's quick denial.

Rhodes was around forty and unmarried, he recalled. He suspected the blonde, Rebecca, had her eye on him.

"Don't reckon I know enough about the murder to say." Both women visibly flinched, apparently not caring much for his plain speaking. "I'm told there's bad blood between Bent Langley and Hammel. Don't know why it would carry over to shooting down a kid though."

Rebecca's pug nose wrinkled in distaste. "Can you think of any reason to shoot a child?"

Actually, Shay could. Depended on if the child was shooting at him. As he remembered, young Billy Bonney had only been around fifteen or sixteen when he started in shooting folks. "Anybody heard if the boy had a weapon?"

"A saddle shotgun. Still in the scabbard," Ruth said and Shay wasn't a bit surprised that she knew. "So it wasn't a shoot-out if that's what you're thinking. I'm afraid you have it right, Mr. Billings." She took a breath. "Cold-blooded murder, a threat meant to drive the Langleys out of the country for fear all their boys will be killed."

"It won't come to that," Rebecca said.

Ruth shook her head hard enough that an ill-secured lock of hair escaped the clasp holding it at the nape. "The way rumors are spreading, I wouldn't be surprised to see local warfare break out, Becca. Look at what's happened in less than a week."

Shay broke into what was looking to become an argument between the women. "What has happened, aside from the Langley boy being killed?" Who better to ask? Natural-born gossip-mongers, they seemed a great deal better apprised of the situation than he was. Or that young hand of Bo Cobb's either. What else did they know?

Ruth gave her sister a hard look. "For one thing, the Fremonts have sold their ranch—lock, stock and a thriving garden patch—to Marvin Hammel and already taken the train to Montana. The Scotts are gone and the Richardsons are trying to negotiate a deal. And Deputy Schlinger resigned and went to work for Bud Knowles."

The Fremonts lived—had lived—closer to Hammel than any of the others, aside from Scott.

"Well, sh—" Shay stopped himself from cussing just in time. "Why'd Schlinger go and quit? What's he doing for Knowles?"

"He's bartending in the Barefoot Saloon or so I hear. Rumor is that he couldn't put up with Rhodes's lackadaisical shenanigans anymore. Shenanigans means defending the Hammel takeover of the river and doing nothing about it."

Rebecca was quick to dispute this. "Hush, Ruth. We don't know truth from lies. And I don't

41

know that it's Sheriff Rhodes's responsibility to patrol the river anyway."

"Huh! Who else's would it be? He's responsible for upholding the law inside this county." Ruth popped the lines again. "Anyway, why don't we know truth from lies? I guess I trust Mr. Schlinger's judgment of character more than I do Sheriff Rhodes and if he says Rhodes washed his hands of the deal, then I believe him."

Apparently being twins didn't include their minds working the same, Shay thought. And he had to agree with Ruth. Distrusting Rhodes, he hadn't voted for him in the last election and if Schlinger would run for sheriff this fall, he'd bet money Rhodes would be out. Even Hammel couldn't throw the election that far off.

His brow puckered into a frown. Or could he?

Rebecca was staring at him. "Whatever is the matter, Mr. Billings? Do you have a pain?"

Although Shay shook his head, he thought maybe he did. It was a relief, though a short-lived one, when they reached the cemetery a few minutes later.

The preacher from the Methodist church officiated at the funeral, a service that dragged on far longer than a person might expect considering the brevity of the life involved. As Shay had reckoned, just about everyone within thirty miles attended except for the woman at the bridge.

This, causing more than a little consternation, included Marvin Hammel, driving up in his new 1901 Pierce-Stanhope motorcar, all dark blue paint and shiny brass. It was only the second automobile Shay had ever seen, the first being T. T. Thurston's Ford delivery wagon which he'd had to help dig out of the mud earlier that spring.

Anyway, Hammel had taken the precaution of bringing his wife and a couple girl children along with him, possibly to forestall a protest at his presence. They all wore black as if they were the chief mourners, the women with their faces hidden behind lacy parasols.

Mrs. Hammel sent her girls, carrying between them a big basket covered in a white napkin, over to the tables where food was laid out for after the service. They set it at the front, then scurried back to the automobile.

The Hammel presence struck Shay as an insult. Evidently, it did to Langley and his family as well. The Langley men, and Shay included the two remaining boys with their father, gazed at Hammel with murder in their eyes. Pinky Langley turned her back to them, refusing acknowledgement, but he saw the tears leaking from her reddened eyes.

Mutters rose loud over the preachifying every now and then, like when the reverend said something about God's will and how vengeance was His. Shay stopped listening about then and watched the attendees, many of whom were doing the same.

Rhodes, also an uninvited attendee, strutted around the perimeter of the gathering watching for trouble. Or maybe looking for a reason to cause some. Shay doubted the sheriff prevented any. More than likely the lack was due to Pinky insisting her boy's burying go off without violence. That and the presence of so many other women and children.

When the preacher finally dropped the first handful of dirt on top of the pine coffin, Hammel and his females left, moving off with the phufft, phufft of the motor car's engine.

After they were gone, the women, quiet and somber, gathered at tables arranged under the trees to set out a potluck meal.

Shay almost laughed when, by accident he was sure, Pinky managed to dump the contents of the Hammel's basket onto the ground and then step in it. Cookies. He saw Ruth snigger behind her hand and Rebecca shake her head sorrowfully.

The men stood a short distance away, faces and voices serious, in the meeting John Johnson had called Shay to attend.

Richardson spoke first, his voice low and sounding sort of worn out. "I'm selling to Hammel. Didn't want to but I had no other choice. Stevens over at the post office told me about a place up north. It's going cheap enough I can buy it free and clear with what Hammel is paying. My wife and girls don't like the area but what else could I do? Listen to my cattle bawling as they die of thirst? Sheriff Rhodes says there's nothing else I can do."

"We oughta get us some dynamite and blow Hammel's dam to kingdom come. And him along with it." The firebrand speaking, and Shay wasn't one bit surprised, was young Art Langley whose face was flushed and angry.

"Don't let Rhodes hear you say so," Bo Cobb said, nodding toward the sheriff who was approaching the group on bowed legs.

Bent Langley, his face lined and tired, put his hand where his gun butt would've been had his wife allowed firearms at the funeral.

"Easy, Bent." Shay touched his friend's shoulder. "Listen to Bo. I'd say we'd best keep our opinions to ourselves until Rhodes leaves."

Bent's teeth ground together but he nodded.

Rhodes, as usual, was full of his own importance. "Break it up, fellas. Ain't going to be any fighting or bad-mouthing here. This is a funeral, not a mob meeting."

What an ass, Shay thought, watching young Arthur Bentley's face.

Bo scowled down at the shorter sheriff. "Unless you make it into one."

"Watch your tongue." Rhodes cocked a thumb

45

towards town. "I got a hoosegow just waiting for troublemakers."

A hoosegow shared with the city marshal but Shay guessed a jail was just a jail.

"Reckon free speech is part of a citizen's Bill of Rights," Bud Knowles said.

Shay thought it was the first amendment to the U.S. Constitution Knowles was talking about but he wasn't about to make a correction. Mainly because he didn't think Rhodes knew either and he didn't plan on spoiling Knowles's argument. He saw Schlinger's eye twitch and figured he'd caught that, too. The former deputy also remained silent.

The rest of the men nodded. "Not if I say it ain't," Rhodes said.

Schlinger was shaking his head. "You can't unmake the law, Elroy. Try and a recall might be in your future. Pretty sure the governor would be interested in what's going on hereabouts."

Mention of the governor nudged Shay. "A letter to the governor telling him about the doings here wouldn't come amiss, Schlinger."

"You worked for him once, didn't you, Billings? Why don't you write it?"

Shay thought about it. "All right. I will." Couldn't do any harm, that's for sure.

"Don't be hasty, Billings," Rhodes said. "Stir up trouble and you'll find you got more than you can handle."

It was Art Langley who had the best idea and had no qualms about voicing it. "Why don't you leave now, Sheriff. We're burying my brother today and we don't need you here. You ain't a friend of ours. This gathering is for friends."

Shay nodded along with the others. To his relief, in the face of the cool reception, Rhodes gave in and did the smart thing for once. He retreated.

Rhodes caught up with Shay before he'd gotten a half-mile out of town. Shay had missed out on escorting the Inman sisters to their cut-off. Now, with Rhodes bearing down on him, he almost regretted it. He'd stopped for a drink, a toast in salute of Joseph Langley and his short life, with some of the others.

"Billings," Rhodes called when he was still some way off. "Wait up. I'd like a word."

Shay could tell the meeting was no accident. What he hadn't bargained for was the moment of unease that swept through him. He should've brought his handgun, he thought, scanning the hills around as though looking for a band of cutthroats. Releasing his Winchester Model 1892 carbine from the saddle scabbard was a little cumbersome if he was in a hurry.

Although the errant thought came to him, he'd trust cutthroats as soon as he would Elroy Rhodes.

Shay hesitated a moment, then said, "Whoa, Hoot."

Hoot stopped.

"What do you want?" Shay asked as Rhodes pulled his horse, a flashy sorrel, to a halt beside him.

"Want?" Rhodes tried on a grin. "I don't want anything, Billings. Actually, I'm about to do you a big favor."

Shay wished he hadn't eaten so much of the funeral food. It set heavy in his belly all of a sudden.

"You are?" He failed to keep the disbelief out of his voice. He didn't believe Rhodes capable of doing him a favor—not without a bigger one in return.

"Why, yes. I am," Rhodes said. The sheriff gave him a look. Unpleasant. Even so, that grin came again. Unless, on second thought, it was a sneer.

Shay waited without speaking.

After a few seconds, voice harder now, Rhodes started his spiel. "Marvin Hammel sent me out to have a talk with you," he said. "He's got a proposition."

Shay admitted to some curiosity though only to himself. "What proposition?"

But Rhodes didn't come right out with it. "Marvin told me he'd paid you a visit. Said he was impressed with your place."

Hoot chose that moment to stomp a hoof, pawing at the road. Eager maybe to get on home.

From the self-conscious way Rhodes mentioned Hammel's first name, Shay knew he wasn't in the habit of thinking of the man as Marvin and didn't call him anything but Mr. Hammel—to his face.

"Marvin said he liked the improvements you've made at the bridge, too. Said he's willing to pay a little something extra for the work."

Shay, who'd been studying the road ahead, sat a little straighter. "What does that mean? 'Pay something extra for the work'?"

"He's making you an offer for your ranch," Rhodes said as if he thought Shay was slow and stupid. "It's the bridge he wants. Says the land isn't worth a great deal when you consider how much he owns already. And even more when he buys these other men out. I figure you'll want to jump at the chance to make a profit." He named a figure $500 more than Shay had paid for the place five years ago. A hundred dollars a year for his backbreaking labor.

Then Rhodes added, "Of course, this all depends on you forgetting about writing any letters. What goes on hereabouts has nothing to do with the powers that be in Olympia."

Anger sizzled through Shay like water percolating in a coffee pot. They thought the paltry offer was enough to buy him off?

Not to mention Hammel's and Rhodes's erro-

49

neous conclusion about the bridge. And he wasn't about to enlighten the sheriff. No, sir. Not until he'd talked to the woman.

On the other hand, he didn't mean that exactly either. He'd talk with her, all right, if he managed to meet her face-to-face again. But he wouldn't ever tell the sheriff about her. Let him find out for himself.

Shay's attention came back to Rhodes who, with a faint smile showing beneath a pencil-line mustache, was waiting for Shay to jump at the chance to sell out at the pittance he'd named. Unless he knew what Shay's answer would be, which he likely did.

Shay touched Hoot with the toe of his boot, causing the horse to jump ahead. "Tell Hammel I ain't for sale," he said over his shoulder.

"You better think again, Billings," Rhodes said as Hoot shouldered past his sorrel. "Everyone is for sale if the price is right."

Shay didn't look back.

CHAPTER 4

January had separated last night's cream from the milk and was churning butter when she spied Shay dropping his five cents in the slot. The dasher stilled as she watched him. Pen, lying in the shade, rose to her feet but January said, "Stay, Pen," and the dog obeyed.

Pen gazed longingly after the man as he disappeared over the hill and maybe January did, too, although she'd have denied it. He'd been polite yesterday. More so than she, and the sound of a human voice had stirred her.

A pleasant voice, she admitted, with a gentleness to it she liked. She also liked how Mr. Billings spoke to his horse who seemed to understand his words. He looked good, too, with his brown hair and dark eyes, and though he needed a shave, he wasn't hirsute. A little thin. Perhaps his wife wasn't much of a cook.

The thought of his wife gave her a funny feeling, one she didn't know how to describe.

One thing about Mr. Billings, he hadn't tried any of those tricks people used to do back in Missoula. Their favorite had been acting like they were picking something off the ground when all they wanted was to get a peek at her face which, out of habit, she kept hidden within the depths of her bonnet. She was wise to them though and almost automatically "turned the other cheek." Nothing for them to gain there.

Gain? What was ever the gain in rooting out secrets to humiliate someone? She'd never understand.

With her butter stored in the spring house down by the river until she could sell it at the store in town, January spent the rest of the morning hoeing. It was a futile attempt to get ahead and keep ahead of the weeds. The soil was rich here along the river although the many rocks were a problem when it came to cultivating. As time allowed, she was collecting the rocks and building a rock fence in the pasture over the hill, constructing it stone-by-stone out of the five- or six-inch ones. Eventually, she hoped to build a real house there and the fence would not only mark her yard but form the house's foundation.

She'd loaded a lowboy with rocks when, mid-afternoon, a small dust cloud rising above the road warned her of a traveler moving at a fast pace. The dust gave her time enough to stable Ernie, her mule, and hide the lowboy inside the barn. A handful of oats in the manger kept the mule busy and quiet. Then she called Pen and they made their way through the passage she'd set up to her quarters. Through the part that wasn't booby-trapped.

Any unwelcome intruder who tried to follow

her in would be sorry, taking into account two batches of two-by-sixes ready to drop on their heads and rusty nails much in evidence. January considered the drum that had sticks attached to a cog as her pièce de résistance. As a last resort, there was a shotgun. As for Pen and herself, they entered the single room she occupied with no trouble.

The room was cozy. Dim right now, being on the shady side of the barn. She went to the peephole that gave her a view of the bridge.

After an interminable time, one in which she knew any rider should've made it from the ridge to the ford, she motioned Pen to stay put and went out to one of the other watch-posts she'd set up around the barn's interior. The first one faced onto the road leading from town.

Frowning, she craned her neck as though to see over hills and around corners—all of which didn't do a particle of good. But when she crossed the yawning barn floor around the edge where the worn planks wouldn't creak, from another vantage point, she caught sight of a man and horse sitting amongst the brush at the edge of the timber.

Just sitting there, watching her place or maybe just the bridge.

It wasn't Shay Billings and Hoot. Nor was it the rider who'd come to warn Shay about the murdered boy. Not that man on a jumpy red horse from three days ago or the one before that either. All of whom had crossed the bridge and headed toward Billings's ranch.

She had no idea who it could be. But he was carrying a rifle in his hand, not stowed in the saddle scabbard.

January hardly breathed as she watched. Five minutes passed and she heard Pen snoring in their room. Then another five before the rider set spur to his horse, a mostly white and black medicine-hat pinto, the top of whose head seemed to disappear in the shade. They climbed the embankment up to the fill where she'd reset the bridge posts and went on across, the rider urging the horse into a lope once they were back on the road.

But she saw they weren't on the road. Not exactly. And it struck her as odd that the rider kept the horse on the verge where the dust rising was minimal. Like he didn't want to be seen.

And he neglected to pay her toll.

Back in the barn, the mule was still hitched to the lowboy. Finished with his oats, he'd become a bit restive. She needed to get him out of the barn. She figured they were done hauling rocks out of the open field for the day. That rider and the way he had sneaked up to the ford then kept out of the road proper gave her the creeps. He'd headed towards the Billings's ranch but that didn't mean he wouldn't spy on her, too.

"Whoa there, Ernie." She spoke softly to the mule as she came around the side of the lowboy and picked up the reins. "Time to call it a day, yes? Let's move this load over to the fence."

But first she retrieved Pen and the old Colt .38 that had belonged to her father, pausing to take another look around before stepping into the open. With Pen leading the way, she didn't relax until they were beyond sight of the barn.

Beyond sight but not beyond sound.

She'd just finished pushing the rocks she'd gathered into a pile more or less where she'd need them once she began mortaring when she heard the sharp crack of a rifle shot echo across the river. Another followed a few seconds later.

January straightened with a jerk and Pen, who'd been stretched on her belly watching, scrambled to her feet.

"Did you hear that, Pen?"

The answer seemed obvious. The dog stood staring off across the creek into the distance, the hair on the back of her neck standing erect.

January froze, gazing about, listening and trying to judge where the shot had come from. After maybe a minute, a flurry of dust rose on the road the stranger with the gun had taken only a half-hour ago.

Pen growled, gathering herself ready to charge off. January grabbed the dog by the scruff.

"No. Stay." She threw herself down behind

the pile of rocks and hugged Pen to her. Seconds later, the pinto came into sight. The horse was running full tilt, the rider leaning low over its neck, apparently unaware of the mane slapping in his face. They didn't slow even a little for the bridge or the barn, sweeping past with the rider's legs pumping as he spurred the horse. And they sure didn't stop to deposit coins in the toll box.

January didn't mind a bit about the lost nickel. Especially when, about the time she'd just gotten to her feet, another horse came trotting down the road in the tracks of the pinto.

A gray horse.

Hoot.

Riderless.

A bright splotch of red painted the saddle and ran down Hoot's shoulder. Another splotch colored the horse's gray hip.

January ran, Pen soon outpacing her. They all three came together at the bridge.

CHAPTER 5

Shay never knew if it was Hoot's gray ears twitching or some sense of his own that warned him to move. A sudden twist to the left may have saved his life but it didn't keep him from getting shot.

The bullet slammed into his back, burning like a lightning bolt before boring a hole under his arm as it exited. Then Hoot jumped and kicked like a rodeo bronc and Shay lost all control. Weak and nerveless, he dropped from the horse's back like he'd been swept off by a giant's fist. The fall so startled the horse that when Shay landed almost directly under his hooves, Hoot jumped straight up. When he touched ground again, he turned and sped back the way he'd come.

Not that Shay was aware of any of this, having whacked his head on the hard ground and knocked himself out cold.

As for Hoot, he slowed down to a trot before he crossed the bridge which allowed January to come close enough to call, "Whoa, whoa there, Hoot." Miraculously, the horse stopped and let the woman and the dog catch him up.

Shay didn't know this part at the time though January told him later.

In his next aware moment, the dying sun

shining into his eyes nearly blinded him and pain so bad he almost wept overwhelmed all else. He cried out like a baby when he tried to lift a hand and brush away the soft, slick thing slobbering all over his face.

His hand dropped to his side. "Dammit, Brin," he muttered.

He had no way to know his muttered words at least proved to January Schutt, as she dropped to her knees beside him, that he was alive. Or that January thought Brin must be his wife's name.

But Shay did hear her say in a sharp, bothered tone of voice. "Pen, leave him alone."

Pen? Who, he wondered, was Pen?

Then a wave of pain took over and he didn't care anymore.

January shuddered as she peered down at Shay. He lay on his left side, facing into the sun. Blood ran from the hideous wound in his back and when she tilted him for a better view, she saw where the bullet had exited under his arm. She gasped and closed her eyes, hoping the gory sight would disappear.

It didn't. When she looked again, it was all still there.

She didn't exactly know what to do. Try to give the man aid? That went without saying. But then what? Should she jump on Hoot and ride to Mr. Billings's ranch for help? There was certainly no way she could get the man into the saddle even if he woke up and tried to help himself.

Besides, Hoot might have something to say about that. Although the graze across the horse's rump wasn't bad, he was still jumpy and the wound probably hurt. Not a good time to break him to riding double.

But she couldn't leave Billings lying in the road, that's for sure.

A travois. That's what she needed.

Or better yet, the lowboy. The idea struck like a bright light. She'd left poor old Ernie hitched to the vehicle as she ran after Hoot. She could bring him here and roll Billings onto the lowboy if she drove off the side of the road where it sloped down. She'd take him to her barn since she had no idea how far it was to his ranch. It could be miles and it was only a half-mile to the bridge and the barn.

And then she'd go to town for the doctor. Or maybe to Billings's ranch. To his wife, this Brin.

Dread filled her at the thought of mixing among people.

"No choice," she murmured aloud. "No choice."

But first she had to stop the bleeding. Or try. Pulling her overly-long, overly-sized shirt—it had originally belonged to father—from the waistband of her trousers, with the aid of a pocket knife she ripped about six inches from the bottom. Making two pads out of it, she pressed one under his arm and one against his back. Sacrificing her long bonnet strings, she hacked them off and used them to wrap around the bandage. He groaned as she pulled them tight. Groaned more than once.

"Don't you worry, Mr. Billings. I'll be back in a wink." Rising to her feet, she spoke to him on the off chance he could hear and realize she was trying to help. "I'll leave my dog with you for company."

She gathered Hoot's reins and clambered into the saddle, careful not to touch his rump when she swung her leg over. "Pen, stay. Guard."

Pen wriggled, not liking the order, but as January kicked Hoot into a lope, she obeyed. Lying down beside the man with a grunt, the dog went back to licking his face.

At home, January found Ernie had wandered almost back to the barn, the lowboy perforce dragging along behind. That was fine with her. It cut a few minutes from the trip. Tying Hoot to the rear of the rig, she raced into the barn and through the interior to her secret room where she gathered a couple blankets, some clean rags for bandages more absorbent than the ones made from her shirt, and filled a jug with water.

Back outside, she jumped aboard the lowboy.

"Walk on," she told Ernie. A little impatient with his plodding pace, she shook the lines over his broad back. He quickened his stride though not by much. It took far longer to get back to Billings than she liked.

Pen yipped a greeting on their return and it seemed to January that Billings's eyelids flickered. His eyes didn't stay open until she drove Ernie and the lowboy into the ditch beside him, the traces rattling and wood creaking. The activity seemed to rouse him.

Before she tried to move him, she reinforced the bandage and held a cup of water to his mouth.

Shay swallowed down a couple sips, hardly choking at all.

"We're going to roll you onto the lowboy, Mr. Billings. Are you ready?"

"Roll?" Shay repeated, as if he'd never heard the word before.

"Or scoot." To her own ears, January sounded apprehensive. Of course he couldn't roll. What had she been thinking?

His dark eyes closed again. "Yeah. I can scoot."

But as it turns out, he couldn't. Not really. At the first shift of his shoulders off the ground, he blanked out again. And stayed that way while January rigged a sort of harness and stretcher combination with a loop to attach a rope. She and Hoot, good cow pony that he was, then tugged Billings onto the lowboy without more damage.

Much more, at least, the increased blood flow from his wounds being scarcely noticeable.

Shay stayed unconscious until they reached the barn when it became a matter of getting him inside. She ended up driving Ernie, lowboy and all, into the barn and simply leaving Shay lie. By the time she situated Billings with blankets and a fresh bandage, unharnessed and unsaddled the horses, and closed up the barn, it was almost dark.

Although she hated the process, as she knew even a glimmer of light could be seen for miles, she lit the lantern.

Chores still needed done. Her cow needed milked and the animals bedded down for the night. She needed to eat some supper as well, having worked hard during the day.

But supper had to wait. When she checked on Shay before going into her hidden room, she found the new bandage wet with fresh blood.

"Dammit," she breathed. Too loud maybe, as he roused again.

He stared up at her. Although it was dark enough in the barn that she knew her features must be obscured, she turned away from him.

To her surprise, he recognized her.

"Sorry, ma'am. Looks like I might need the doc," he whispered.

"Yes. I'm afraid you do."

She'd have to go to town. No choice. There were those words again.

"Your wife . . ." she started, then stopped.

"No. Just Brin," he said. "And Hoot. Where's Hoot?"

"I've taken care of your horse. He'll be all right." Puzzled, she frowned. Just Brin? But she couldn't think of that now. Billings sounded weaker than he had out on the trail and he needed a doctor. Leave him much longer and he'd bleed to death. She knew he wouldn't last the night without help.

And maybe not then. But she had to try.

She found another bonnet, one with strings attached, tucked her tail-less shirt more firmly into her trousers and saddled Molly, her buckskin saddle horse. On her way out, she checked on Billings one last time.

"I'm going for the doctor now, Mr. Billings," she told him. "I'll be back as fast as I can. I'm leaving my dog here with you."

A whisper of response didn't exactly reassure her. A whisper or a grunt . . . or the moan of a dying man?

Mounting Molly, January urged her horse into a fast running walk, the mare's best gait. The safest one, too, for traveling the rutted road on this moonless night. Stars lent barely enough light to keep them on track.

To January, the trip seemed to take forever. What if Billings bled out and died inside her barn?

Not that he'd be the first man to do so.

The vision of Shay Billings's gray face, pain etching deep lines along the side of his mouth, haunted January. Once, she urged Molly to greater speed until the mare broke into a lope. A stumble put a stop to that.

A little more than two hours later, they arrived at the edge of town.

It wasn't really so late, January realized, perhaps a couple of hours until midnight. Lanterns hung outside the town's two saloons, a beacon for carousers. A bordello masquerading as a rooming house showed light in an upstairs room. The small hotel had a lamp glowing in the front window while a yellow light shone in the newspaper office. Mr. Ritter probably working through the night to get the Friday edition out on time after waiting to write up the Langley boy's funeral.

At least the streets were empty. Relieved by the lack of people, January guided Molly down Main Street until they came to the first corner. They turned left and went on a couple blocks. By the third block, they were almost out of town again. The doctor's office was in an ell addition attached to the last house, a blocky building in need of paint. Dr. James LeBret, said a faded sign.

Dismounting stiffly, January followed a well-worn path to the ell's door. There was a notice telling her to pull the the cord dangling from a small hole in the jamb and that a bell would ring, summoning the doctor.

January yanked. Sure enough, a bell pealed, a sound heard faintly through the door. She waited a minute and yanked the cord again.

"I'm coming, I'm coming," a grumpy-sounding voice called. Footsteps came closer.

January raised the bonnet which she'd allowed to bump loose against her back on the ride to town, pulling it tight until it hid her face. The door jerked open as she adjusted the brim.

"Well?" the man standing there said. He wore eyeglasses that had slid down on the end of his nose. "Who's sick?" Then, as he apparently noticed the caller was a woman, "Or having a baby?"

"I need help," January said. Her voice was huskier than usual and she swallowed. She'd heard those exact same words before, years ago, only it had been her father saying them. Swiftly, she added, "A man has been shot. He needs help right away."

The door opened wider and the doctor beckoned her forward. "Who is it? Where is he?" He peered over her shoulder as though expecting to find the patient waiting for him. Finding no one, he shut the door and set match to another lamp wick.

January flinched from the light. "Do you know Shay Billings? He's the man who's been shot.

He's under cover right now at the . . . the barn at the Kindred Creek crossing."

"I know Shay," the doctor admitted. "Don't know why anyone would want to shoot him unless—was it an accident? He's a good man. That old barn though. It's abandoned and has been for ten years or more. But if he was close there, it means he was almost home. When did the shooting occur?"

"About three, maybe four hours ago. He's bleeding badly." She described the wound best she knew how.

Doc rattled off more questions as he ushered January into the lobby part of the ell. A few chairs sat in an untidy semi-circle around a desk. Beyond this room was another, the doctor's surgery. The open door showed a sturdy waist-high table with a six-armed lamp hanging above it. Cupboards, some with glass fronts, provided a view of vials and jars of crushed herbs and powders. Banks of drawers filled the lower cabinets.

The mere sight gave January the willies, her memory of the last time she'd been here all too clear.

The doc kept knives in the drawers. Saws, too. And needles already threaded and packaged to keep them clean. Doc was a stickler for cleanliness, she remembered, but not much for treating pain and fear. She'd been a child then, hurting terribly and afraid. Afraid most of all. She hoped the doctor had forgotten.

"Bleeding badly, eh? Hope we're not too late. Three hours is plenty to drain a man dry." Doc's dire prognosis drew her from her preoccupation as he bumbled around the room stuffing items into a black leather bag. "Were you there? Who did the shooting?"

"He was ambushed not long before dark. I have no idea who did it except the shooter rides a paint horse. Mr. Billings was only semi-conscious when I found him and couldn't talk. I hope . . ." She shut off what she'd started to say. "I think the bullet passed through. There is an exit wound."

Doc paused to squint at her. "Exit wound, eh? You know one when you see one?"

January, with a twitch, ducked her head, hiding from his scrutiny. "I heard two shots from the . . . from where I was but he was hit only once. His horse got skinned by the other. Please, doctor, he needs care. We should hurry."

He reached for a jacket hanging on a coat tree by the door and jammed a bowler onto his head. "I'm ready. Just gotta harness the horse."

Long practice had made the doctor efficient. They were soon making their way through the quiet town to the road. A man had come to the Barefoot Saloon's door as they passed and stood looking out at them. He didn't say anything and neither did the doctor but January felt the weight of the man's gaze.

In plain fact, Doctor LeBret didn't say anything at all for a long time, to the point January wondered if he were dozing and simply letting his horse follow the road. When he did speak, she gave a startled jump.

"I beg your pardon?" she said.

He shook the reins over his horse's back and didn't look toward her. Not that he could've seen much as it was so dark a lantern wouldn't't've come amiss. One held out front on a long, high pole to light the way.

"I said, are you the Schutt girl, come back home? You are, aren't you?"

Shock twizzled through her. So he did remember that awful night. She'd hoped he wouldn't.

"Yes," she said after a while. "I am she."

"How long has it been. Ten, fifteen years?"

"Thirteen."

She saw his head tilt toward her. "How did you guess?" she asked.

He huffed out a half-laugh. "You're wearing a bonnet in the dead of night, one that covers your face. A bonnet from thirty years ago and way outside of fashion even then. I figured you must be hiding something. When you mentioned the Schutt barn at the crossing, it couldn't help but bring back memories." His shoulders hunched. "Did I do that bad of a job?"

"You ought to know."

Her terse reply earned a raucous snort. "I took every care, but you needed skilled nursing. Soothing salves and frequently changed dressings. Instead, you disappeared. My patient gone. Did your father . . . ?"

"We were on the run. You know that. You called the sheriff down on us yourself." The bitterness in her voice surprised her. After all these years, the pain was still raw.

"I called the law in when it happened, yes. I had to. I told the sheriff the crime was the one against you. I told him Schutt probably started the fire and shot himself when he realized what he'd done. Tried to do. Your dad should've stayed and faced down those who questioned him."

"He was protecting me." January's shout made both horses jump, the doc's buggy leaping ahead.

"And if he'd stayed," LeBret said when he'd soothed his horse, "we'd have proved Wilhelm Schutt deserved to die."

"Really?" She didn't believe him.

"Really," he said, so firmly she almost did believe him—for all of thirty seconds.

She couldn't bear to hear anymore about that night. "I'm riding on ahead," she told the doctor. "I'll be in the barn." Molly broke into a trot as January chirped to her, then into a lope until they had left Dr. LeBret behind.

January slowed the horse then, continuing on at a more sedate pace.

She found Pen sitting in front of the barn when she got home. The dog rose to her feet and shook her black fur. January, casting a worried look at the animal, thought she seemed awfully subdued.

Sliding from Molly's back, she led the horse into the silent barn and into a stall. "Hell," she whispered to the dog, "he isn't dead, is he?"

CHAPTER 6

The lantern had run out of oil while January had been gone, leaving the barn's interior pitch dark. Fortunately, Pen made a good guide and January knew her way through the maze well enough even without a light.

She found a lamp in her hidden room and struck a match to it. The doctor would need something to guide him in and at 12:30 in the morning, she didn't expect anything but coyotes and owls to be hanging about to wonder at the beacon in the darkness.

Dread hurrying her heartbeat, she carried the lamp over to see if Billings was still alive.

He was.

His eyes opened as she knelt beside him. It wasn't until they widened that she realized her bonnet lay against her back instead of sitting on her head and shielding her face. January turned away so fast her neck popped. Had he seen? She pulled the bonnet over her tangled hair and adjusted the brim.

"The doctor is right behind me," she said when she could speak. "He'll be here in a few minutes."

"Thanks," he whispered. "Thought you weren't coming back except you left the dog."

"It's a long ride into town."

"Water?"

"Right here." Propping him up far enough to swallow without choking was more of an ordeal than she liked. Smears of fresh blood dotted her own shirt when he'd managed a cupful. To her relief, Dr. LeBret wheeled into the barnyard a few minutes later and immediately set to work.

"I need more light," he snapped out. "Boiling water. Clean rags. Got a decent bed for this man? He needs something better than these dirt-covered boards."

These were the easy things although January wasn't so sure she appreciated having to open her room and move Billings into her own bed. Which wasn't really any more than a cot sporting a thick pallet. At least it was garbed in clean sheets and warm blankets.

"It'll do," Doc said. She'd led him through the maze to show the way. His gaze took in the paint job meant to confuse the eye, the building that promised deception, the secret route to her hidden room.

"Clever." He nodded. "I remember your dad being a master builder before he came back here after your mother died. He built Hammel's house, as matter of fact, and it's still considered the best in town. Built Mayor Fogel's house, too. And put the ell on mine. Where is he?"

January was building a fire in the small pot-bellied stove that had once warmed the room where they kept the tack. Her hands stilled on the kindling. "He's dead. Has been for over three years."

Doc opened his bag, spreading his surgery supplies out on a three-legged table. "Then who did all this?" A wave of his hand took in the room and beyond. "And the bridge? I've been hearing about a bridge."

"I did."

"You? By yourself?"

"Yes." She gave an unladylike snort. "What's the matter? You never heard of a female builder before?"

Doc whistled. "I guess I never did. It must mean you're a strong woman which is good because the two of us are going to carry Billings in here. I'll take his shoulders; you take his feet."

"Won't a stretcher work better?" January asked.

Doctor LeBret grunted. "Would if we had one."

"I've got something that will work as well."

"You do?"

"Yes."

January didn't want to brag but she kept such a thing on hand, an implement she'd found useful while alone in her carpentry endeavors and in building the bridge. A simple board platform kept level via triangular braces and set atop two wheels connected by an axle, it worked well. With one person in front pulling and one in back pushing, their patient soon lay on January's bed.

Had Billings remained conscious during the process of moving him onto the cart, he no doubt would've been grateful.

Doc LeBret said it was the best thing for the patient. To remain unconscious, he meant. He pushed his spectacles higher on his nose and adjusted the lamp. "More light," he demanded. "I'll need to probe the wound, make sure no shirt fibers remain in there. Don't want infection setting in."

"Won't the blood have cleansed the wound?"

"Maybe, maybe not. Is that water hot?"

"Soon." The fire was crackling. For extra light, January resorted to setting out the candles she kept around in case her supply of coal oil ran low.

LeBret grumbled. "Damn things, candles. They blow out just when you need them the most. Be glad when we get electricity here—if we ever do."

Inclined to agree, January used her entire store. Set together, they worked well enough although she never wanted to think back on what they revealed as Dr. LeBret performed surgery. The stitches he placed at last, leaving a drain tube sticking out under Billings's arm, was the least of it.

Doc yawned hugely as he repacked surgical instruments in his leather bag. He followed January through the barn to where his horse and buggy stood waiting out front.

"I'll try to get back this evening," he said, looking up at a sky turning milky gray with the coming dawn. "If his skin feels hot and he starts tossing around, bathe him with cool water. Speaking of water, make sure he drinks some even if you have to wake him up to do it. He needs the water to make more blood. Feed him beef or chicken broth to build him up. Try to keep him still. I don't want the drain tube coming out."

"All right." A frown creased January's brow. Sometime during the operation, she'd allowed the bonnet to fall back. After all, what did it matter if the doctor saw her and the results of his handiwork from years ago? "Who is going to tell his wife what happened? She must be terribly worried by now."

"Wife?" LeBret gawked at her. "When did he get married? Last I heard he lived out here alone and had every spinster female in the country after him. And maybe some females who aren't spinsters."

"He mentioned someone. A name."

Doc shrugged. "Well, Miss Schutt, I don't know what Billings has been up to. I suppose whoever shot him had a reason. Maybe you'd better go over to his place and see if anyone is there. Won't take you but an hour or so. He oughta stay asleep that long."

"Shouldn't you do it?" The thought of meeting

75

anyone new set January's stomach atremble.

"You're his closest neighbor. And I can't spare the time. I may have more emergencies in town."

"I've done my part," she insisted.

Doc settled a level gaze on her. "And you need to do this much more." Untying his patient horse from the post, he climbed into his buggy and popped the reins. They headed for town at a good clip then, leaving her waving dust away from her face.

January had a notion he'd be asleep before he'd gone a mile.

He was no more than out of sight when it struck her she should've asked him to keep this nighttime emergency call to himself. If whoever ambushed Mr. Billings found out he hadn't finished the job—

Well, she'd best be prepared.

When she saddled Molly again, she wore a pistol strapped around her waist, uncomfortable as could be, bumping against her hip and leg. The proximity did nothing to reassure her.

"Stay, Pen. Guard."

Crossing the bridge, she headed in the direction of Shay Billings's ranch.

Doc was wrong about one thing, January discovered a good three-quarters of an hour later. She was bound to be gone longer than an hour. Definitely into the "or so" part of the equation.

She couldn't help being impressed by what she saw when at last she reached Billings's property. It had been easy enough to find, just a couple more miles farther than she'd bargained for. A section of new fencing marked the boundary. A sturdy rail gate barred the trail onto the ranch. He'd put a name to the place, with Billings painted vertically down the gate's anchor post. Helpful.

January hopped off Molly and slid the rails back far enough to lead the horse in, replacing the rails as soon as she was through. Mounting again, they plodded on. They must be getting close, she thought, growing a little impatient.

Just over a low hill to her right, she heard the rushing sound of the creek, still running high as it tumbled over a fall of stones. A bit farther and the creek came in sight. There were a half-dozen white-faced beeves standing at the water's edge, sprigs of fresh green grass hanging from their mouths as they chewed. Coming upon a cross-fence, she discovered a pasture of maybe twenty acres with ten—she counted them—mares with foals. Apparently, Billings specialized in horses rather than cattle. Spying her, the mares came running to the fence to greet her. Molly nickered in return.

At last, ranch buildings appeared. A small house—more a cabin really as it was built of logs—a barn maybe five times bigger than the house, and a privy sitting on a mound of freshly turned earth. Over by the barn was a chicken coop surrounded by fine wire fencing right up against a shed where she spotted a harrow, a mower, and other implements. A wagon with removable sides was parked alongside the shed. Beyond that, she saw where he'd started a small orchard of a few pear, plum, and apple trees.

But the dog was what stopped her.

The large brindle hound sat in the middle of the yard looking at her.

"Hello," she said. "Who are you?"

The dog's tail thumped a reply.

A bird called as it moved through a tuft of tall grass over by the manure pile. Then a deep quiet settled over the ranch yard. Only the far-off gurgle of the creek and the susurrant whisper of tree tops in the breeze broke the stillness. The cabin door remained closed. No smoke rose from the chimney.

Except for the dog and a few big white chickens scratching within the wire pen, the place appeared deserted.

January eyed the hound. Got down from Molly and led the horse forward.

She stopped maybe ten feet away from the dog, the brindle dog, who watched her out of sad eyes. The connection was easy to make.

"Are you Brin?"

The hound stood up, ears lifting a fraction.

"I think that means yes." Extending her open hand, January held it out. "Well, Brin, I'm January and I've got news about your man. He's been shot and is bad off. He's laid up at my place. Hoot is there, too. Hoot is fine."

Another name the dog recognized. She paced forward a cautious step or two, poking her nose toward January.

January gazed around. "It appears all is well here. Whoever shot Mr. Billings evidently is leaving the place be." She looked down at Brin. "I'm sure you're a good guard dog but you shouldn't be left alone. I think you'd better come along with me. You can keep Mr. Billings company while he recovers."

Brin cocked her head, attentive to the words.

If he recovers. January pushed aside the insidious little voice in her head, refusing to listen. He would make it through. She'd see to it.

Brin accompanied her as January checked the yard. The creek ran through a corner of the pasture so she needn't worry about water for the horses. The chickens were another matter. Filling containers, she scattered some corn she found in the barn and hoped for the best.

Then, figuring Brin was used to her by now, she patted the dog and gave the long ears a good scratch. "Ready to go?"

She mounted Molly. "Come, Brin." None too certain the dog would obey, after a few steps, she looked back. The dog sat in the road again. Waiting.

January's sharp whistle pierced the morning air. "Come, Brin," she said, the command plain. This time, to her satisfaction, Brin got up and followed Molly.

When they reached the place where January had found Billings, the hound stopped and howled. The eerie sound raised the hair on her arms and even made Molly's ears twitch. The dog sniffed, walked about and seemed as if she were on a trail for a while. January didn't know if she was tracking Ernie and the lowboy with Billings aboard, Hoot, or the man who'd done the shooting.

It probably didn't matter.

When they reached the bridge, January dismounted and caught Brin, tying a rope around her neck before they got to the barn. Evidently the hound had worn a collar a time or two because she didn't fight the rope. The walk seemed to have tired her and January suspected that like Pen, she was an old dog, both of them gone gray around the muzzle.

The meeting between the two dogs went well. A few warning growls, Pen coming over a trifle territorial. Nothing a gentle reprimand didn't solve. By then Brin had caught Billings's scent and tugged on ahead, following her nose into the secret room.

Billings lay just as January had left him, leaning slightly to his good side to take pressure off the wound. At some point, he'd roused enough to drink a little water, the tin mug she'd left on the table by the pallet being half empty now. His face was flushed a bit and when she lay her hand on his forehead, it felt warm though not blazing. His breath came in little puffs and she guessed he was in pain.

She'd make an infusion of pussy willow bark, she decided. Maybe that would help the fever. She already had a wild lettuce concoction for pain.

Brin flopped down beside him and stuck her nose in his hand.

"Brin," he muttered, his lips barely moving.

January's heart fluttered a little, sensing a bond between the man and dog similar to the one she and Pen shared.

She sacrificed one of her chickens that afternoon, beheading it with one quick blow of her ax, holding it by the legs and dipping it up and down in a pail of scalding water. Afterward, pulling the feathers was a breeze. Soon the smell of rich chicken broth filled the room, causing not only the two dogs to sit at her heels but rousing the man.

Turning, careful not to step on any dog toes, she saw Billings toss the blanket aside and try to rise. "Hungry," he said. "Is supper ready, Ma?"

The sentence dismayed her. Oh, not the part

about being hungry. She had no doubt his stomach was as empty as an overturned bucket. But the rest. Ma, he'd said, like a querulous little boy.

Silenced, she stared at him. He stared in return but after a few seconds, she concluded he wasn't really seeing her.

Just as well, she thought, suddenly aware she'd forgotten to adjust her bonnet. She pulled it up around her face, regretting the necessity. She never intentionally wore it when she was cooking and certainly not when she was alone. And she'd been alone a lot.

What wasn't just as well were his eyes. Rather nice eyes. She'd particularly noticed them, even at their first meeting when he came to tell her about the funeral. They were a dark gray color she'd never seen before on anyone. And right now those eyes were glazed over as though he were looking through frost. His face, though merely warm before, was now flushed and hot with fever.

She didn't think he actually saw her. Or not her as January Schutt. Maybe as his mother.

Mr. Billings had decidedly taken a turn for the worse.

"Rat scat," January muttered, starting forward to persuade him to lie back.

He fought her ministrations but only a little before weakness overtook him.

The next couple hours involved bathing his face and neck with cool water, forcing more water down his gullet, and persuading him to drink quantities of the feverfew infusion. He didn't like the herb's taste judging by the faces he made and, truthfully, it didn't seem to help much.

Even so, she kept treating him as best she was able.

Much to her relief, Doctor LeBret showed up just before dark, calling her name from outside the barn so as not to startle her.

Not that he would've anyway since she'd been on the lookout for him this past hour. Both dogs had warned her of his imminent arrival as well.

She motioned him to pull his rig into the barn, out of sight of any chance passersby.

"How's the patient?" Doc clambered from his buggy, his legs stiff.

January shook her head. "He's in a lot of pain, I'm afraid. His fever is up. I've been trying to bring it down but nothing seems to work, not even the feverfew."

"And his wound? Is he still bleeding?"

"Some. Not a lot, but I'm worried."

"I see that." Doc huffed out through his nose. "Well, let me take a look at him." He motioned for her to lead the way through her maze to the hidden room.

"Did you find a Mrs. Billings?" he asked.

"No, no Mrs. Billings." She pushed open the

door and gestured him inside. "But meet Brin."

Doc gazed around the small room. "Who . . . ?"

"The dog. The brindle hound. That's Brin. Mr. Billings belongs to her."

Doc's bellow of laughter awakened Shay. A good thing, really, since it meant his fever had broken.

CHAPTER 7

A visitor came around the next night. A visitor besides Dr. LeBret, that is. This one arrived late at night when Shay, January, and even the dogs were sleeping.

Shay slept less hard than the others. Every time he moved, pain from the wound in his side brought him fully awake which is why he heard the soft tinkle of a harness bell.

Or he thought he did. Eyes open into the dark, he held his breath listening for the sound to come again. It was almost as though an errant breeze had stirred in the worn out tack left hanging from pegs driven into the barn walls. He'd lost track of time and how long he'd been here but he'd had a few hours to familiarize himself to the sounds and vagaries of the decrepit building. The chime of harness bells didn't mean wind. It meant the barn door had opened and that meant by a human hand.

He lay immobile, barely breathing, his body stiff and still. Just listening. The chime didn't come again. He heard nothing more. Too much nothing. He imagined a sound as slight as a foot padding through dust.

Brin lay curled at his feet. Shay believed her asleep, too, until the dog's head suddenly lifted.

She sniffed, got up and stretched before turning to face the door.

The woman slept on a pallet a couple yards away.

"Miss." Shay's low voice barely carried the distance to the woman's makeshift bed. He still didn't know her name.

She didn't stir. He didn't blame her as he figured she was probably worn out. She worked constantly, doing this, doing that in her garden, in the field, running in to tend him. He'd seen her through the open door, building a table out of barn wood she told him were salvaged planks from ruined parts of the barn. Planing and sanding and oiling and gluing and fitting.

Whoever heard of a woman building furniture? Beautifully crafted furniture, at that.

Shay felt around around the cot. Where the hell had she put his gun? Somewhere out of reach, he guessed, as he couldn't find it.

"Miss," he said again. Brin, clever dog, shook herself, padded over to the woman and stuck her nose in the woman's ear.

The woman sat up like she'd been poked with a stick.

"Miss. Shh." Shay hoped she wouldn't speak. "Where's my pistol?"

The woman rose to her feet in a fluid motion, soundless in her strength. She'd gone to bed wearing her trousers and men's shirt but without the previously ever-present bonnet. No matter. She made only a slender silhouette in the dark anyway.

"What's wrong." She leaned over him. "Has someone broken in?" Her voice was as quiet as his.

"Yes. I think so. Brin thinks so."

Apparently, she had no problem in finding her way around the room even in the dark. A second later, he felt the butt of his pistol being pushed into his hand.

"I'll be back," she said. "Don't shoot me."

Then she disappeared.

"Wait," he said, too late. He neither saw nor heard her go, only felt her absence when gone. She left him and Brin in the room by themselves. Her big black dog went with her, as silent and stealthy as she.

Shay threw back his blanket, gasping with pain as he heaved himself into a sitting position, his back braced against the barn wall. Sweat ran down his face.

"Wait," he said again but it was he who waited, his .44 in his hand.

January figured she could put the blame for the visitor straight onto Dr. LeBret. Except whoever had invaded her barn wasn't a visitor but an intruder. In consideration of the Langley boy's murder, Doc probably reported the shooting to the authorities and she feared the news had gotten around by now.

Whoever had sneaked into her barn had no doubt followed Dr. LeBret on his rounds and been led here. It'd been simple. January had no doubt the intruder was the man who'd shot Billings in the first place, back to finish the job. The idea did nothing to reassure her.

In fact, she thought as she maneuvered her way through the maze between the big empty barn space and her hidden room, she almost wished she hadn't heard those two rifle shots. Or observed the man on the pinto make his panicked yet furtive escape. Or gone looking for Billings when his horse ran past with an empty saddle.

Pen a faithful shadow behind her, she stopped beside a scattering of broken stall boards. They offered clear passage if one knew the way which she and Pen did. If one didn't know the way, they were an almost impenetrable obstruction.

January stood still and listened. Ahead of her, someone, a man, breathed heavily. He suppressed a string of curses as he banged a knee or a shin into the lowboy she'd left standing in the middle of the barn floor when she'd transported Billings to the barn. Although she'd never before heard some of the words he used, she recognized that they weren't words suitable for proper society.

A match flared and the man's face, all shadows

and highlights, appeared beneath a wide hat brim. Not a tall man, she judged. One sweating and nervous, his body odor so rank with unwashed youth she could smell him at a distance. He held a long-barreled pistol in his hand and she thought he might be smiling.

Did he think cold-blooded murder was going to be easy?

Not if she had anything to say about it. She'd thwarted him once by saving his victim. She'd do it again.

The tiny light the match provided showed him moving away from her. Then, in the next second, the light went out. He kept walking until a grunt indicated this time he'd probably walked into one of the pillars holding up the loft. They were still strong after all these years. Stronger than the stall divisions and walls separating sections in the cavernous space which had become ramshackle. Some of them even dangerous to the unwary.

He lit another match and, turning, came toward her again, the gun held out in front of him.

It almost made her laugh. Didn't he know all the lit match did was destroy his night vision and pinpoint his location? Which, from her point of view, worked in her favor.

January touched Pen's head. The dog had a lot of age on her. Too much to be the guard dog she'd once been. January hated like anything putting her companion in danger. Only as a last resort. Only if she had to.

Pen may have had other ideas. She was on alert, shifting stance, her muscles tight under January's hand.

January's muscles tightened, too. She didn't like waiting for him here, so close to the passage into the inner room. Better to meet him half-way.

Pen paced forward with her, the two of them drifting like black ghosts. January took up a position in front of the lowboy where the wagon's tongue stood upright.

The intruder's second match burned out. He dropped it with a snap of scorched fingers, a spark showing its path. The afterimage on her retinas marked his whereabouts.

Pray he doesn't set my barn on fire.

The man inched closer, moving cautiously now, and was almost near enough for January to touch when he struck a third match. Two glowing green orbs showed in the match's flickering light. His breath hissed in on a startled jerk. His gun lifted even as Pen emitted a hoarse growl gaining in volume. He fired at where the orbs had been only seconds before but Pen had vanished. She came out of the dark beside him, leaping for his gun hand.

January pushed the wagon tongue down in front of him when he tried to run. He stumbled over the long wooden piece and fell to his knees. Pen's strong teeth glommed onto his gun hand and he screamed as though all the hounds of hell were on him. The pistol dropped to the ground and discharged, the bullet going who knows where.

In truth, it may have seemed like the hounds were loosed as Brin, shut up with her master, howled a mighty complaint from the hidden room.

January swung her pistol at where she thought the man's face might be, connecting with a meaty thud. He screamed again, tearing himself away from Pen as she closed on him. Scrambling up from his crouch, he ran for the barn door as if devils dogged his heels.

At least his sense of direction remained true.

Finding the exit, he slammed open the barn door, ricocheted off the jamb with a force to nearly knock himself down, and ran on. A horse whinnied. Seconds later, hoofbeats pounded the earth, fading as the horse galloped away.

January watched the horse's mad sprint, laughing a little as Pen dashed after them barking. The horse had been white with dark patches. The same horse the man who'd shot Billings had been riding. She was certain of it.

The myriad questions invading her mind weren't as funny as seeing the intruder in flight. Why was he trying to kill Billings? Now that he knew where to look, would he be back? Would he bring help next time?

She guessed the last question sort of answered the one before it.

The barrel of Shay's .44 rose, wavering as a slight figure slipped through the door.

"It's me," the woman said, "don't shoot." Her words, spoken in a normal tone of voice, came near to making him do the exact opposite.

He recovered just in time. "I won't." Relief allowed his gun hand, already shaking under the strain of holding steady all this time, to go slack. Or if not steady, he admitted to himself, at least it'd been available. "Is he gone? I heard shots. You all right?"

The effort of speech brought him near to exhaustion.

Light burgeoned as she set a sulphur to the lamp wick and just for a moment he saw her face. Then she turned away and her features were lost to the dark side of the room. He felt bad when she stuck one of those ever-present bonnets on her head and yanked it down by the strings.

"He's gone. Pen and I are fine. He became a bit disoriented in the barn and shot at Pen. He missed, needless to say." The dog panted up at her at the mention of her name. "That was the first shot you heard," the woman went on. "The second is when he dropped his pistol and it fired accidentally. I picked it up after he skedaddled and have it right here. I hoped you might know who it belongs to."

She showed him the pistol. Pearl-handled grips, decorative etching on steel, extra long barrel. Fancy and expensive.

Shay's eyes narrowed. "Not a typical ranch hand's gun."

"No. I thought not. I expect someone is bound to recognize it. Then we'll have the identity of the man who shot you and he can be put in jail." She stowed the pistol in a beautiful little wooden box of the type Shay associated with pirates' treasure chests.

Not that he knew a damn thing about sea-going pirates. Could be land pirates were another story. He'd seen that fancy pistol before and he didn't like where this was heading.

He blinked and found the woman staring at him from under the bonnet brim. "You know who this pistol belongs to, don't you, Mr. Billings? I wonder, are you thinking of the same person who rides the flashy pinto? White with a black heart-shaped patch on his chest?"

Wincing against the pain of moving, Shay set his pistol aside and let himself down on the cot. Answering took too much effort. Her questions would have to wait. He'd answer them though, tomorrow maybe. It wouldn't be fair not to. Because from the looks of things, they were both in a bad situation, she as deeply as he. All through no fault of her own.

Not his fault either. The thought did nothing to ease him into sleep.

Sometime the next morning, the hollow clunk of hoofbeats crossing the bridge awakened Shay. It took more than one horse to make that much noise and whoever was riding them didn't stop to pay the toll.

He looked over to where the woman had been sleeping but she was gone. Her dog lay in front of the door, nose on forepaws, eyes alert. Brin sat beside his cot. She gave a little whine when she saw he was awake. Flailing about with the hand on his good side, he found his pistol lying beside his pillow. That she'd left it there for him must mean she expected trouble.

Where was she? Why had she left the dogs inside with him? The barn and this little room were quiet as the grave.

Shay, in no small battle, propped himself against the wall like he'd done last night. The effort turned him into a sweating, exhausted wreck. Still, considering he managed it at all, he figured he'd made some progress over the last couple days. From what he could see of his bandages, he hadn't bled any from his struggles last night or just now.

He sat there, wishing for the strength to get on

his feet. Either that or wishing she'd come back. What if something had happened to her? Why was it so damn quiet, inside and out?

Those horses, those riders. Who were they? Where had they gone?

His horses and his cattle, his house and barn, all were wide open and unprotected. What if those riders had been a band of rustlers bent on stealing his animals? What if they tore down his house? Would Rhodes do anything about it?

He suspected it might depend on who'd done the stealing. And the tearing. And why.

An hour or so later, the horses returned. Shay didn't even think about them being different from the ones he'd heard earlier.

Whatever had been done was done and there wasn't one single thing he could do about it. Not right now.

But later, he promised himself. Later.

Holding that thought, the world turned upside down and he toppled over in a heap.

In spite of, or perhaps because of, the upset during the night, January awoke before dawn. Too restless to sleep longer, she and the dogs slipped from the room, Brin having quickly learned the route by following Pen. They left Billings fast asleep, pained little puffs of air rising from between his lips.

Outside, she fed the horses, including Hoot in

the roster of critters, and milked her cow, leaning her head against the bovine's warm flank. The milk, run through the separator and strained into metal cans, went to cool in the homestead's original springhouse down by the creek. The structure was still in good condition though lacking actual ice. The stream ran under the rock building, a piece of good construction engineered by her father years ago. Sharing a rock-lined canal, it sat right next to the pumphouse, an ingenious set-up for filling the animals' watering troughs and irrigating the garden. After thirteen years, all she'd had to do was buy a new pump and with a little tinkering, the system worked as good as new.

She was spreading grain for her chickens when the memory of doing the same for Billings's critters came to her.

Someone had a vendetta against him, that much was clear. Did he even know why? Would that transfer to his possessions? To his animals? To his house?

Her gaze went to the knoll, to the long abandoned burial plot she was probably the only person on earth to remember.

"In making war," one of the dead had said, "if you destroy the enemy's home, you'll destroy them." She didn't know if that was true or not but it made sense. And if it was so, the person—or persons—out to get her neighbor probably would try annihilation of his home and livelihood next. Especially as the sneaky so-and-so from last night had failed at whatever he'd meant to do.

He'd meant to make sure Billings died.

The situation didn't set well with January. She figured she'd better do something about it.

Which was why, without even stopping for breakfast even though she was hungry as a wolverine in spring, she saddled Molly and took the road to his place. She hardly thought twice about leaving the dogs to protect Billings.

At the last minute, she took Billings's carbine from the scabbard of his saddle.

"Just in case," she whispered to herself, hardly daring think "just in case" of what.

Having seen her coming, his ten mares with foals were lined up in the corral nuzzling at an empty manger when she rode in. A metal trough held only a few inches of water covered by green scum. Evidently the horses were his spoiled babies, accustomed to personal attention.

She set about doing the usual chores. Leading Molly into the barn, she pumped water into the trough, grained the horses, spread corn for the hens and collected some eggs. She'd take them home and fix him some breakfast, she thought, her own stomach growling. Make a cake . . . but no. She had no oven although it was surprising what she could manage with the cast iron Dutch oven.

The next step caused her to hesitate. Billings's shirt had been a rag she threw away, saturated with blood and shot full of holes no amount of stitching could mend. He still wore the britches he'd had on. Also covered with blood and dirt. The man had begun to stink.

So she went inside his house.

The interior was clean and tidy. A cup, plate, and fork lay on a towel were he'd put them after washing. A kitchen range provided both heat and cooking surface, its presence a surprise. She wondered, a spasm of pure envy overtaking her, if he baked since his stove did have an oven. The main room contained a table and a couple of kitchen chairs in one area and a couple easy chairs with a roll-top desk centered along one wall. A highboy chest opposite the door was a commanding presence in the room. It seemed a fancy piece for a man living alone. A leftover, perhaps, inherited from a relative.

A door in the far wall led her to a bedroom. A few clothes were folded and placed on a shelf. A small mirror hung above a commode where a wash basin with a floral trim and a plain white pitcher waited. There was a bed, the blankets pulled taut, another chair, and strangely, a book-case overflowing with well-worn books. Nothing led her to believe he was anyone besides a hard-working rancher and certainly not wealthy. But not poor either.

Why would anyone want to murder him?

January had just chosen a shirt, trousers, socks, and some sawed off long-johns when she heard hoofbeats pounding up from the main road.

Jerking her bonnet closer to her head, she peered out the front window, glad she'd tied Molly in the barn out of sight. Her pistol was strapped to her waist and she'd carried Billings's rifle into the house with her.

Dust swirled as four horses drew to a halt in the dooryard. Over by the coop, chickens clucked and yodeled a greeting, drawing one man's attention. The man had a black eye and bruised cheek, a bandage around one hand, and he rode a medicine-hat pinto with a heart-shaped black patch on its chest.

January's stomach did a flip-flop.

She was caught in the house with no way out except the front. Unless . . . the bedroom had a window in the eastern wall but was it big enough to allow her to escape?

The man with the bandage drew a pistol, smaller than the one she'd taken from him during the night. Quick as a striking snake, he fired off a shot. The head disappeared from one of the chickens. It flopped and flapped its wings around the pen, blood spouting from the headless neck.

Two of the men laughed.

Anger leapt into living flame along January's nerves. A chicken now. The horses next? The cattle? No, no, no. But how was she to prevent it?

She scooted back into the bedroom. Thin as a fence post from all her hard work, she fit through the window, never mind the small patch of skin and blood she left on the sill. A few seconds later, Billings's carbine in her hand, she dropped to the ground at the back of the house.

Gunfire erupting from the front had her trembling as she crept to the corner and peered through a large service berry bush growing there. Spreading the branches, she saw only two chickens were left alive and one of the men was taking aim to finish them off. The pen was practically afloat in blood.

Her eyes narrowed; her teeth gritted. This was the outside of enough. These men were worse than a bunch of Viking vandals.

Poking the carbine barrel through the branches, she fired off a shot, hardly caring where it went. A man's hat went flying. So did the man since the horse he was riding startled into bucking like a raw bronc. It was the pinto.

"Hellfire!" one of the other men yelled, half off the saddle and reining his own horse in a circle.

"Git," January shouted, deepening her voice. "Next bullet is in you instead of your hat."

Ducking behind the house again for cover, she levered another cartridge into the chamber and waited to see what they'd do.

CHAPTER 8

Under other circumstances, the men's and horses' didos might've been funny.

A peek around the corner showed the man she and Pen had bested last night flopping on the ground trying to keep his pinto from running off without him. The one spinning his horse was losing his seat a little more with each gyration. He finally stepped off before total humiliation overcame him. The third man had his bay under such a cruel grip the horse's mouth gaped wide open. January felt bad about that.

The last of the bunch had kept some kind of control of his mount, a bright sorrel, although the horse was crow-hopping and tossing its head in an effort to join in the hijinks.

The man on the bay said something to the sorrel's rider although January was unable hear what. Apparently an order of some sort because the man on the sorrel sort of gathered himself and, after one false start, shouted, "Put down your rifle and give yourself up. I'm the sheriff of this here county and you're under arrest for attacking an officer of the law."

The sheriff? Surely not. January's lip curled in scorn. She stepped farther back into the concealment of the house.

"You're the sheriff?" she yelled back. "An

unlikely story if I ever heard one. You don't act like any sheriff I ever heard of."

"Get her," the one on the bay said.

January took the precaution of moving a few steps to the side. "Sheriffs are elected to keep the peace not cause a ruckus. You and your gang better leave before I shoot a few of you."

"Dammit, Rhodes, run 'er outta there." The man on the bay palmed his handgun and fired, emptying the revolver in her general direction.

A bullet whizzed past, slamming into the corner of the house and biting off a chunk of the wood. January was unsurprised by his reaction. As soon as she finished speaking, she'd dropped to the ground behind the corner of the house where the rock foundation provided protection. When she'd counted off six shots, she got up and ran to the other end of the building.

Stepping around the corner there, she aimed the carbine and squeezed the trigger. The first bullet raised a cloud of dust between the two men on the ground. The second hit between the bay's forelegs, sending him into a wild dance of protest. The rider, trying to reload his pistol, dropped a handful of cartridges onto the ground where the horse trampled them into the dirt.

"You men are trespassing." She jumped back into the house's shelter. "I'll be reporting this to the real authorities and sending a telegram to the governor. I'll tell him there's someone here impersonating an officer while he and a gang of outlaws wantonly destroy a man's property."

"I ain't—" the man started but January cut him off.

"In my world, mister, even chickens have value and you've just destroyed this man's property. Now leave."

"You can't—" he said but she'd already fired off another round and whatever he was saying got lost. His horse decided it'd had enough and took off for home. The sorrel finally succeeded in claiming the bit and followed. With some difficulty, the man with the bad hand mounted his pretty pinto and the other finally regained his seat. They were only a few yards behind the leaders by the time they all reached the road. A dirty gray hat, a little pummeled by horses' hooves, lay abandoned in the dirt.

January sent the last bullet in the carbine speeding after them. It served to keep them going if they'd been inclined to argue further. A good thing, too, she thought wryly, seeing she had no more ammunition.

Her innards felt like they'd been picked up and rattled all together by the time she recovered enough to get back to business.

Once astride Molly—Billings's clothes tied on behind the saddle and two dead chickens, gutted though not plucked, in an empty grain bag she'd found in the barn and hung from the saddle horn—she couldn't quite decide what to do next. Ambush, she figured, was a real danger from thugs like the ones here today. After all, there'd been two people gunned down already that she knew of. She'd best have a care.

Which meant an extra hour's ride across the hills to a spot she knew had a good ford across the river. It put her on the far side of her place and several more miles for Molly to cover.

Better be safe, she thought, although she didn't like leaving Billings alone for so long. What if, in their anger, those men stopped at her barn? What would they do? Could Shay Billings protect himself? She doubted it. He was pretty much defenseless.

She reminded herself he had his pistol, not that she found the thought reassuring.

He's weak. He might not awaken. The dogs. What if they shoot the dogs?

January chirped to Molly and thrummed her heels against the mare's sides.

They made good time on the way back, January having asked the mare for more speed than usual. Finally, they crested the rise above the ranch yard where she stopped and surveyed the barn. The place seemed untouched in its dilapidated condition. No fires or guns spewing bullets or any dead men or animals. Not as far as she could tell, at any rate. Nevertheless, she approached with caution.

It turned out to be unnecessary.

Pen came to greet her, tail wagging with joy.

January's heart almost stopped. "How did you get out?"

The dog, unconcerned by the worry in her mistress's voice, went nose to nose with Molly and sniffed the bag with the chickens.

"Yes, you'll eat well tonight," January whispered to her, pulling the dog's ear. "No bones. Just real meat."

Pen licked her chops as if she'd understood every word.

January wended her way through the maze to the hidden room. She found Billings propped against the wall, slumped to the side in an uncomfortable looking heap. His eyes opened as she came through the door.

"Where have you been?" His voice was hoarse but at least he could speak. "Are you all right? I heard horses go by here and you were gone. I was afraid they meant trouble. That they—" He struggled upright, sweat breaking out on his forehead.

So he'd been aware of danger, both his and hers. But . . . he'd been worried? She couldn't remember the last time someone had worried about her. Her dad, but he'd been dead for over three years now. There'd been no one since.

"I'm fine, Mr. Billings. I'm used to taking care of myself." She extracted the chickens from the sack. "I've been over at your place, checking on your livestock and finding some clean clothes for you. I hope you don't mind but I entered your house."

"Checking my livestock or just killing my chickens?" He had his eyes on the carcasses, the white feathers being distinctive. Her chickens were a plain gold color and good egg layers.

"Oh, I didn't kill these. But after they were dead, I didn't want them to go to waste. I'm afraid those men you heard had a destination in mind when they passed here, along with a plan of destruction. A couple of them decided shooting the heads off your chickens is a fine pastime. I'm sorry I wasn't able to stop all the carnage."

"My horses? My cattle?" Billings's lips turned white as he attempted to raise himself higher against the wall.

"Just the chickens. The other livestock are all right—for now." She settled her bonnet closer around her face and bent to examine his bandages. "Let me help you lie down, Mr. Billings. I can see you're in pain and in need of rest."

"My horses." He ignored her offer of help. "You said they're all right for now. What do you mean?"

"I mean I wouldn't be surprised if those men returned, possibly bringing more of the same ilk. I don't know who they are but our intruder from last night was among them." She knelt beside him, carefully turning her head to the side. "Who are these people? Why are they doing this, Mr. Billings? What have you done to bring them down on you?"

Billings stared at her as if she'd been speaking Japanese. "I don't know," he said after a while.

"You don't know who? Or you don't know why?"

"Both."

She tugged at his bandage, securing it more firmly in place. "You'd better figure it out, sir, before they kill you. And me. They'll be coming after me as well, after today."

"You?"

She huffed out a short laugh. "I told you I stopped the carnage. What I didn't say was that it required the use of firearms. They didn't like backing down.

"I was terrified that when I got back here I'd discover they'd gotten in and killed the dogs—and you, of course—on their way past."

A pained smile touched his face. "Thanks for laying my pistol handy. I was ready for them. We wouldn't want anything to happen to the dogs or the barn—or to me." Deliberately, a crooked smile turning up his lips, he added her words. "Of course." He sobered again. "They didn't stop."

Satisfied his bandage was in place, January rose

to her feet. "A cause for celebration, Mr. Billings, I assure you."

"Shay," he said.

"Pardon me?"

"Shay. That's my name. I'd be pleased if you'd skip the Mr. Billings part and call me Shay."

"Oh."

"What's yours?"

"Mine?"

He was looking at her with those funny-colored eyes. "Your name. I'm thinking you've got one. Something other than The Woman Who Lives in the Barn, or maybe, The Woman Who Built a Bridge." He came off sounding exasperated.

Even then she took a few moments, thinking what to do. He hadn't lived here thirteen years ago. Maybe he wouldn't even recognize the name. Or care if he did. Maybe nobody talked about what'd happened anymore. Doc had seemed unconcerned but he'd only tidied up the aftermath. He hadn't been the one to run—or maybe die.

She made up her mind. She owed this man the courtesy of telling him her name, no matter how reluctant. "I'm January Schutt. You may call me January." Because the fewer times her last name was bandied about, the better she'd like it.

"January." He grinned. "Bet you was born in the winter."

She hid her smile in the depths of the bonnet. "Bet you'd win your bet."

January busied herself fixing breakfast, noticing he managed to lift the spoon to his mouth just fine. She plucked and prepared his chickens before going on to the other myriad tasks awaiting her. One in particular relied on her carpentry skills and she didn't know if she was up to it.

Shay settled down and went to sleep right after eating, relieving her of one last chore. As much as she dreaded it, she'd have to tell him the whole story of what had transpired at his ranch. Not right now. Let him recover a bit more. But soon.

Across the field behind the ramshackle barn and hidden from view on the road lay the remains of the house where January had been born. Nothing more than a partial foundation and a few charred timbers were left of her Grandfather Schutt's house. Her father had set it afire on that last night but it had been raining. Apparently the fire had gone out before the oldest part was consumed—not that she'd known this until her return. Neither had her father. The original section had been built of stones hauled from the field just as she was still doing with the intention of constructing her fence and rebuilding the foundation. She wanted the building finished before winter came again. The barn was none too warm with wind blowing through gaps in the siding.

• • •

Two days passed. Each morning when he woke up, Shay decided he felt better and that this would be the day he rose from the creaky cot he slept in. Each of those mornings, although steam still rose from the mug of coffee sitting on a little table by the bed, the woman was gone. She had an uncanny sense of when he was about to open his eyes and made an escape before he caught a glimpse of her. He'd eat the eggs and toast with wild raspberry jam she left with the coffee, then fall back asleep again.

Shay hated being an invalid. And of depending on a fine lady like Miss—or maybe Mrs.—Schutt. He snorted to himself. He didn't even know which title went with her name. January Schutt. It wasn't like any woman's name he'd ever heard before but then he'd never met a female like her before either. A lady living out here, twelve miles from town, all alone. Well, not quite alone. With a dog for company. A woman who built things like tables, and rooms hidden in barns, and bridges over rivers, and . . . didn't he remember her saying she intended on building a rock fence and then a house? A real house?

He'd never considered a woman capable of doing those things. Not ever. Especially a whip thin little thing like her.

Meanwhile, he worried himself sick over what might be happening at his ranch. Miss January was keeping things from him, he could tell, while saying his ranch and livestock were safe. She'd told him last night that whoever those men had been, they hadn't come back.

He didn't see how she could be so certain. If they'd sneaked past here on the other side of the river like he'd had to do before she rebuilt the bridge, she might not've noticed them.

Shay made plans to waylay her when she came in at noon, or maybe this evening at the latest, and demand the news. He remembered she'd said something last night about Doc making another visit to check his wound. Doc would talk to him. Tell him the truth.

Wish Brin could talk, he thought. He'd been noticing the hound had made herself right at home and he was grateful for Miss January for bringing the old girl here from the ranch. The dog would've done her best to defend her home in case those rowdies returned but he'd rather not put her to the test. Which reminded him. Where had she got to now?

"Brin?" Cranking himself up on the cot, Shay sat with his back against the wall, wincing and breathing a little heavy from the effort. "Brin, where are you?"

His voice echoed through the deep silence of the empty barn. After a while, he heard Brin's toenails clicking on the plank floor as she made her way through the maze leading to this room.

The hound's head peeked around the door frame. Seeing him awake, she entered and rested her head on his thigh.

Shay tugged a long ear. "What you been doing, girl? Lying in the sun? Your fur is hot."

The dog was panting, too, and after allowing a few pats, she went over to a large crockery bowl sitting on the floor and began lapping water.

Miss January knew how to take care of animals, Shay thought approvingly. And maybe people, too.

Doc certainly thought so. When Shay awakened from his latest nap sometime past noon, Doc had arrived and Miss January was dishing chicken soup—what else?—into three bowls. Thick slabs of yeast bread smeared with pale yellow butter accompanied the soup.

Shay muttered thanks and licked his chops. He only ever had butter to eat when he took a meal at the restaurant in town. In his own house, he spread rendered bacon fat on his biscuits.

Doctor LeBret interrupted him as he prepared to sink his teeth into the bread.

"Well, Billings, I see you haven't lost your appetite," the doctor said. "That's a good sign. Has the bleeding completely stopped?"

"Yeah," Shay muttered and was glad when the doctor slurped a spoonful of the soup and immediately turned to January.

"You're an excellent cook, Miss Schutt," Doc said.

Shay took note of the "miss."

"This is good soup," Doc continued. "Good bread, too. Who taught you? Not your mother. I believe she passed before you reached an age to begin cooking."

Embarrassed by the question Doc had aimed at him, Shay ignored the banter and concentrated on chewing his bread and hoping he'd learn something about Miss January. Waiting to hear January's response to Doc's interrogation, for that's how the questions struck him, Shay paused with the bread poised close to his mouth before he took a second bite. His belly rumbled. Better to take it slow and give his innards time to adjust.

January simply shrugged. "Dad and I lived in a boarding house run by a widow lady in . . . in the town where we settled when we left here. She taught me. My work proved satisfactory. As I grew up and took on more of the cooking, she paid me a little."

An extra twinge of curiosity tweaked Shay's senses. Was he mistaken or had there been something a little dodgy in the way January avoided saying anything real specific.

Doc must've thought so. He squinted at her. "Your grandfather is long dead and buried, January. The manner of his death doesn't matter anymore. Isn't that right?"

Shay didn't miss January's not quite invisible jerk. But Shay sort of jerked, too. What kind of questions were those anyway? What did they mean to imply? Secrets, that's for damn sure. And now he thought about it, he was surprised Doc knew so much about Miss January's past.

Meanwhile, Doc blathered on. "And your father has passed, too. What's it going to hurt if you tell people what happened that night? It's over and done, right? I guess I'm the only one outside your family who ever knew, or even guessed, the trouble that came before the fire. Most folks figured the old man killed himself. I never told anybody any different."

Doc, to Shay's surprise, sounded plumb annoyed, like he figured he had a right to know everything about everybody.

Shay became even more curious when January gasped in an alarming kind of way. Like maybe she needed a shoulder to lean on. Or maybe for her to cry on because, although she wore one of those ugly, all-concealing bonnets of hers, he thought he heard a rasp in her voice when she spoke.

"If it's over and done, then kindly let the matter drop." Oddly enough, her words came out firm and clear. "I relive that night every time I look in a mirror—which I avoid on principal. I don't need it brought up by outsiders. And frankly, no offense, my family's business is none of yours."

On the other hand, Shay decided, no sympathy required. That was anger he heard, loud and clear.

Placing her still full bowl of soup on the plank counter she used for food preparation, she stepped around Shay's outstretched legs and left the room without another word.

Shay gaped after her, figuring his mouth hung open as about as unattractively as Doc's—except Shay had all his teeth.

He was surprised to see Dr. LeBret's face turn dark under his crop of bushy whiskers at Miss January's plain speaking. Guilty conscience? Shay wondered. Embarrassment? Or was Doc digging for something else? Whatever the doctor intended, Shay found his curiosity running rampant, too. It'd always been obvious Miss January had secrets that weighed heavy on her. Here was proof.

"You gonna tell me what that little showdown was about?" he asked.

Doc, rising to his feet, shook his head. "No. If you can get her to talk to you, I've got a notion she might be soothed but she's right. It's not my place to bring those things up." He opened his medical bag and took out some salve and clean bandages. "Now, let's take a look at this wound of yours."

Shay figured Doc should've minded his own business in the first place.

He thumped the nearly empty bowl down beside his bed. Brin, who'd been waiting and drooling patiently for her turn at the soup, immediately stuck her nose in and lapped up any leavings, including the smell.

Tonight, Shay decided, he and January Schutt were going to have a talk. But only provided Doc didn't torture him to death in the next five minutes by poking and prodding at his wound. He yelped as LeBret yanked away the soggy used bandage.

"Sorry," LeBret said, but so offhand Shay wasn't sure he meant it.

CHAPTER 9

January watered her garden via a drum pump placed within a deep hole in the river, half hidden by the overhanging branches of a big old cottonwood. She'd built a supporting cage for the pump which diverted water via a valve into a shallow wooden trough she'd made, delivering it between rows in the field. A clever shut-off contraption kept critters and debris from the pump itself. None of that meant watering her garden was easy but certainly better than lugging buckets full up from the river.

Late afternoon found her opening and closing gates into the rills. Pen kept her company and lay panting in the shade of a cottonwood grown tall over the last ten or so years.

"I need to invent a mechanism for you to walk on to do this for me," January told the dog as she closed off the final row. She was panting quite hard herself. Mud splatters dotted her face and arms and caked her boots. "Although the way I feel, Ernie might be a better choice for foot power. But at least we're done for the day."

Standing erect, she stretched her back, yanked off the ever-present bonnet and fanned herself with it. "Yeck." Sweat ran down her face.

Stepping deeper into the shade with Pen, she used her shirt sleeve to wipe the moisture away. "What I wouldn't give for a little swim."

Pen got up, went to the river's edge, and lapped water before stepping daintily into the flow.

"Show off." January smiled and followed the dog to the bank where a low spot gave easy access. Maybe there'd be time for a short dip. Her fingers went to her shirt buttons, the top two undone before it occurred to her that with a male guest in her hidden barn room, maybe she'd better check for privacy first. Although with Shay Billings so sorely wounded, it wasn't as if he were able to sneak up on her—even if he'd been so inclined. Anyway, the room was on the other side of the barn.

Nevertheless, she gazed around.

A frown creased her brow. "What in the world?"

The cow was trotting toward home, a full hour before her usual time. Ole Ernie followed, tossing his head like a colt and emitting a loud bray which meant he was upset by something. Birds exploded into the sky from the small grove of trees left standing in the pasture to provide shelter for the critters.

For a second, January thought her heart might stop.

"Oh, no. Pen, come," she whispered. She

touched the pistol she kept with her from old habit.

The dog paddled in little circles, oblivious to January's distress.

"Come." January spoke a little louder. Common sense told her that if she hadn't been spotted before, adding some volume to carry to Pen's ears wouldn't be any greater danger now.

This time the dog heard her. Or at least saw the hand motion ordering obedience. Pen jumped to the riverbank and shook. Water droplets splattered January and she shivered again.

Suddenly, Pen lifted her head and sniffed before pointing her nose toward the pasture and preparing to howl. Time was, the dog would've sensed trouble on the wind long before now.

"Hush." January clamped her hand over Pen's muzzle. "I know. Wait."

But "wait" wasn't an option.

January drew her pistol. There. Movement rattled the bushes where the cow had been loafing. And the birds had risen from Ernie's favored drowsing spot. January squinted, caught the flash of sunlight on metal a fraction of a second before a bullet tore through the tree branches an inch above her head and only a little to her right.

"Sonofa . . ."

She'd become a target. In her favor, the rattling bushes meant she'd spotted the ambusher's hiding place. Pure luck. She snapped off a shot and waited long enough to see leaves shake before she ducked beneath the riverbank's rim. Even at this distance, she heard a pained curse, in turn leading to a flurry of return fire.

Now she'd done it. If the shooter had mayhem on his mind before, now he had murder.

"Down, Pen."

The dog sprawled onto her belly. January did the same, peering over the low edge of the riverbank.

Oh, Lordy. If these were the same men who'd shot up Shay Billings's ranch the other day, they'd be in no mood to let her off easy. Especially if the man with the pinto was along. Or even the one who'd stepped off his horse. Or worse, the man who'd claimed to be the sheriff. Or the one she thought had been giving the orders, who'd mistreated his horse.

If all four of those men were involved, it meant there were plenty to surround her place. These two on the far side of her garden had her pinned down which left two to go after Shay. After the mix-up the other night, they knew he was laid up inside the barn, especially since they'd followed the doctor here. Even supposing Doctor LeBret hadn't given directions on how to find a way through her maze, Billings was in no shape to take care of himself. She had to get back to him.

Lifting her head, January tried to watch the bushes and the trees all at the same time. One of the men must've spotted her shift in position because another bullet raised dust as it struck the bank only a foot away. She ducked down again and stared about. Only one course of action occurred to her.

January raised up, popped off one shot into the bushes, another into the trees, knowing that at this distance hitting anything was doubtful. She moved before they reciprocated which they promptly did, dust and rock shards flying into the air. They probably thought they had her pinned down, what with the river flowing at her back. Maybe they figured she'd be too frightened to move.

They were half right. She was frightened but not paralyzed. Angry, too. Mad through and through, the blood in her veins running red hot with it.

"Come on, Pen." She scrambled along the rocky shelf between the water and the bank, sometimes on her hands and knees, staying low and trying to make herself small. She'd crawl on her belly if she had to. A few hundred feet would get her out of the shooter's probable line of sight and bring her to the corral at the rear of the barn. She'd need to make sure of where the other two yahoos—if they were even there—had taken position before she broke cover and crossed the open patch of ground. If someone was watching out back, she had to dispose of him somehow. The hidden entrance there had to remain hidden. She had no desire to make a run for it and risk coming under gunfire. The latch was tricky and sometimes took a while to manipulate from the outside.

Pen worked as lookout, sometimes ranging a few feet ahead, sometimes a few feet behind, treating their withdrawal like a new game. At last they got to where January planned to cross to the barn.

Taking a chance, she raised her head above the riverbank and scanned the area, first examining the henhouse, then the remains of a tool shed where she remembered her grandfather working at a forge hammering hot steel, sparks flying. At first she thought the way clear until she noticed the way her Buff Orpington chickens were flapping their wings and clucking with excitement. Stuck between her and her destination, the cow and Ernie had stopped and were milling about.

"Well, fiddlesticks." She sat back, catching her breath and resting a knee. Bloodstains corresponding to a painful spot where she'd dragged it over some rocks showed through her canvas trousers. Absent-mindedly, she pressed the cloth against the small wound. "Now what?"

Pen tilted her head one way then the other.

January risked another peek. Only one idea occurred to her and she didn't like it one bit. One of her critters was apt to get shot. Forced to make a choice between the critters as to which she liked best, she chose Ernie. After all, she'd given him a name; the cow was just "Bossy."

"He's in the chicken coop," she said to the dog. "Which gives us a chance if I can climb onto the roof. But he's apt to spot me coming through the corral. At least, he could unless he's really fixated on the barn so I'd better not take the chance. See, if I can get around to where Ernie and the cow are, maybe I can work my way over to the blind side of the coop. Hopefully, I can sneak up and take him by surprise."

Listening to her own words, it seemed there were a great many coulds, ifs and maybes. Yes, and a hope.

Pen stood up.

"No, you stay here, Pen. I don't want to take a chance on him shooting you. If the man in the henhouse is the same one from the other night, I figure he has a grudge against you already."

Pen's tail waved gaily, indicating her lack of worry.

January took a breath, checking her back trail like her dad had taught her. A shot rang out from where she'd been five minutes ago. One of those men still shooting at shadows, she figured. Well, good for him. It kept him occupied.

January looked at Pen and gave the command. "Down. Stay."

Pen's tail drooped. She whined in protest although she obeyed.

January made her way over the top of the riverbank and headed for the coop, creeping as stealthily as she knew how until she came up alongside the cow. Urging the beast into motion, she walked bent over beside Bossy until they reached the henhouse. At the final moment, as the cow rubbed against the side of the small structure, January dashed into its shelter and pressed her ear to the wall.

"What the hell?" a man inside muttered, sounding almost as tense as January felt. "Who's there?" he called out, not very loud.

A boulder, one that had proved too large to move when her dad and grandfather built the coop, stood only inches from the structure. Just as she'd done many times as a child, January clambered onto the rock and from there crawled to the low roof. It was easier now, she found, than it had been then.

The half-door at the front creaked open, masking any small sounds she made. By this time, the cow had ambled away from the structure. Now, as long as the man came around her side, January knew just what to do. If he went around the other way, well, she knew what to do then, too.

She slid her pistol from its holster and reversed it, holding the barrel like a club.

Footsteps crunched dry ground as they came closer, grinding in the bits of vegetation and corn she fed her layers. He headed directly toward her.

January's belly quivered. Crouching low, she watched the man's shadow swell as he neared the corner.

Then he was there, turning in her direction and as he passed below, she leapt on top of him, slamming the butt of her revolver into his head as hard as she could. The steel end knocked his hat off, then bounced hard against his skull. He cried out and she hit him again, this time a resounding thunk atop the head followed by a strike against his neck. The barrel of her gun vibrated in her palm.

He collapsed beneath her and as he went to his knees, she grabbed at the sawed-off shotgun he'd carried thrust out in front of him, pushing it away. Jumping free, she hit him again for good measure until finally he fell, sprawling at her feet.

Dead to the world, she thought with some satisfaction.

Or maybe just dead.

Bright blood flowed where her pistol had broken his skin, flaying open at least one wound. His half-open eyes had rolled up in his head and he lay on his back with both arms frozen in the air as if trying to fend her off. She recognized him. It was the man whose horse had unseated him at Billings's place.

A dry growl wrenched from her throat. Had she killed him?

Well, she hadn't time to care. What she did care about was her neighbor lying wounded inside the barn. And her cow safe to chew her cud another day.

January scavenged not only the man's—in her mind she named him an outlaw—shotgun but a pistol he'd stuck in his waistband and a knife from a belt scabbard; thankful, mostly, when she saw his chest move with a shallow breath.

She dumped all of his weapons out of sight behind the boulder. Him, she let lie.

Thoughtful of time passing, she dashed for the corner of the barn where the roof had fallen in and hung over the outside wall. The area had been showered with debris but that wasn't an accurate picture. January had done quite a bit of work there and now it was her back door, although even she had to stoop to get in and out.

Once she had the latch undone and the door open, she waved for Pen to come. Dodging under fallen timbers, slipping through narrow openings where planks crosshatched the aisles, they soon reached the hidden room.

With evening drawing on, the barn was dark. And quiet. Too quiet? No patter of little mice feet? No buzzing of trapped insects? No settling of dry timbers as they cooled with the setting of the sun?

But the barn proved not to be entirely silent. A board creaked from the loft overhead. She smelled the fall of moldering hay dust. They were not alone in the structure.

January scratched on the door with a fingernail. "Billings, it's me. I'm coming in," she whispered.

She took what seemed to be a grunt as assent. Pushing open the door, she and Pen darted inside.

CHAPTER 10

Shay, shocked that he'd fallen asleep while aware he was under attack, jerked awake with Brin nosing his neck. Grunting with the effort of lifting his arm, he fended her off. "Shoo, Brin, get away. What're you doing?"

A female voice answered. "Trying to awaken you. We've got visitors. I'm afraid they're not here to wish you well."

For a confused moment, he thought Brin had actually spoken. But no. It was his hostess, Miss January.

Shay grunted and with his eyes still closed, levered himself up until he sat propped against the wall. "Where's my revolver?"

"Right beside you."

"Oh." Shay felt around until he touched metal, picked up the pistol and set it on his lap. The box of shells was nearby. He pulled them closer. More awake now, he opened his eyes and watched January who gave a little "oomph" as she barred the door, lifting a heavy two-by-six into a couple of iron brackets.

"You're ready for anything, ain't you?" he said.

"I try."

Her preparations disturbed him. He'd never met a woman like her before, always on the lookout and ready for trouble. What scared her so badly she hid her face and built barriers in a barn? He sure didn't like having involved her in what had turned into a shooting war. She was apt to get hurt and it'd be his fault.

"How many of them are there?" he asked. "That you know of anyway."

"There were four. The same four who killed your chickens, I think. But only three now."

The two-by-six slid into the brackets with a thump. She collapsed onto the lone chair and just sat, sunbonneted head bowed. He wished she'd take the ugly thing off. She was, Shay noticed, all atremble.

"What happened out there?" he asked. "Did you have to shoot one? I heard gunfire."

"No. Worse."

Shay thought maybe he'd heard her wrong. "Worse?"

She shuddered. "Yes. I buffaloed him." She reached for her holstered pistol and drew it from the leather using her thumb and forefinger. Blood stained the dark wooden butt. "But he's not dead. At least, I don't think he is. He was breathing when I left him out by the chicken coop."

She got up and searched out a rag, scrubbing the bloodstains away. "But another outlaw is here, in the barn. Two were out in the pasture. I imagine they'll be along when they discover I'm no longer where they thought I was. Which means we'd better be ready to defend ourselves."

"Yes, ma'am." It appeared to him as though her preparations were all made, taking into account the barred door and her weapons. Those consisted of a shotgun with a scratched up stock and a pistol which, from where he sat, looked like a .38. She had some ammunition set handy, too. She didn't, it occurred to him, have a lot of it and come to think of it, neither did he. He hadn't been expecting trouble on his way home from the Langley boy's funeral, carrying just what was in his belt and a handful of cartridges for his saddle gun. As far as he knew then, no one had any reason to go after him.

It startled him to realize he didn't know of any reason now. But then he remembered Rhodes playing go-between for Marvin Hammel, pressuring him to sell his ranch for a little of nothing. Sell or die. Was that it? But why?

Fresh anger stirred. Rhodes had mentioned Miss January's bridge, too. What was it he'd said? No time to think of it now as a noise from elsewhere in the barn caught his ears.

Looking around, Shay noticed his carbine was missing, probably still attached to his saddle and stored in the barn somewhere. Or near wherever January had put Hoot.

The room was dim as dusk came on. Rays of light entered through cracks high up in the barn's walls. Cracks Shay thought must've made for a right cold winter—or even spring—if she'd been here then. Kind of shamed him to think he didn't know when she'd arrived. He only knew it hadn't been until after Thanksgiving because he'd made a foray into town about then, bypassing this spot and taking the long way down to the ford. The snow on this side of the river had been deep and undisturbed.

They sat quiet as barn mice, each with a softly panting dog beside them until January finally spoke. "Who are these men, Mr. Billings? Why do they want to kill you? What do they think to gain?"

Shay choked on a short laugh, coughing and wincing with the pain to his severed nerves. "Why? I do not know, Miss January, but I figure it's tied somehow to an offer I got to buy my ranch. A right poor offer it was, too." His brows drew together in thought. "Strikes me as part and parcel of young Joseph Langley being murdered, seeing as how Bent got a similar offer a few days before his boy was killed. Hell, they only gave me a couple hours."

"Hours?"

"I turned him down flat. Looks like that ain't what he wanted to hear."

"He, you say. Who is this 'he' you keep talking about?"

"A man who don't make a good enemy. Sheriff Elroy Rhodes."

January jerked erect. "Sheriff Rhodes? That's one of the men who attacked your ranch. Or at least, that's what he said his name was."

"He introduced himself?" Shay didn't bother to hide his astonishment.

"Not exactly. But he said he was the sheriff and another man, one who bossed the others around, called him Rhodes."

"If he admits to being the sheriff, seems he might think you ain't going to tell anybody. And the only reason he'd think you ain't is because—" The slam of wood on wood came from the front of the barn and he appeared to lose track of what he was saying.

Pondering a moment, he said, "I had some visitors over the last few days. You might've noticed an increase of income due to use of your toll bridge."

She shrugged. "Not so's you'd notice. Definitely not getting rich."

Miss January had made a joke. Shay wished she'd take that cursed monstrous bonnet off so he could see her smile. He was sure she had a pretty one and he wondered if she had green eyes or blue eyes to go with her mahogany-colored hair.

Casting the thought aside, he said, "One of my visitors was a feller by the name of Marvin Hammel. Thought you might've noticed him ride past. Either then or in that group of chicken killers."

January opened her mouth to speak but Pen, who'd been lying at her mistress's side, scrambled to her feet. The hair along her back stood on end and she snarled. Seconds later, Brin did the same.

Shay shifted position, lifting his pistol. Resting the barrel on his drawn-up knees, he pointed it toward the door.

"Easy, Pen," January whispered. "I hear them. Wait."

The words no more than cleared her mouth than Shay heard men talking. Oddly enough, the sound seemed to come from outside when he'd thought they'd entered the barn. Footsteps crunched and their interchange became clear as the men stopped right on the other side of the outer wall.

Shay shifted his pistol's point of aim.

"How the hell did the woman get involved anyhow?" one said. "And what possessed her to drag Billings here, to a rundown abandoned barn like this? Savin' his worthless life. Don't even make sense. Who is she and where did she come from? Where does she even live? You got any idea?"

If Shay had to say, the speaker sounded right put out at poor Miss January.

"I don't know anything about her. Never seen her before," a second one said.

The first speaker snorted. "You haven't seen

her now. That get up she wears makes for a damn good disguise."

"Yeah, but LeBret knows her. You can be sure of that, the nosy old coot. I can get her name out of him."

"Just don't rough him up too much. Might need his services yourself one of these days." There was a pause, then the same man said, "In fact, forget it. We'll all be better off if the woman and Billings simply vanish, as of today."

"Best thing that could happen," the second man agreed.

The first man's voice deepened. "See to it then. Do it yourself. Don't put it on Edgar. He's a weak link; willing, but panics at the wrong time and leaves a mess just like he did with the Langley boy. You do it clean and bury them deep. Now then, if my boy hasn't run off, he must be inside and there's no back door to this place. They can't get past us. Let's go get 'em."

Their conversation faded as they tromped off.

Flabbergasted, Shay said, "Well, by gum, if that ain't a confession, I never heard one."

January swallowed audibly. "A confession as well as a statement expressing their intention to murder us both. Now, if we only knew who they were, names to name besides the sheriff. Doesn't do much good if you can't point your finger in the proper direction." She went over and put her ear to the door.

Shay was surprised at how calm she sounded.

"Oh, I know who they are," he said. "As they're no doubt aware. Reckon it's one reason why they want to kill me so bad."

"Well, who—" January never finished her question because right then the first of her booby traps went off outside the door.

Pen pointed her nose and yowled in competition which even at that instant brought a smile to Shay's face. Brought a question to his lips as well. "What in the Sam Patch is that?"

A big rat-a-tat-tat noise, for certain. A clatter that sounded like the roof was coming down. Or maybe an army was on the march. Must've scared the feller who'd run into whatever caused it to lose his wits since a Gawd-awful racket of shooting and yelling broke out in two corners of the barn.

Someone shouted that he'd taken a bullet, then a voice roared, "Stop shooting! Stop shooting, you damn fools. Wait until you've got a target. And make sure it ain't one of us."

Sound advice although it took a few moments to have any effect. Even then, while the shooting stopped, the hollering didn't.

January turned from the door. "Well," she said after a little pause while she seemed to catch her breath, "that worked better than I thought it would."

Shay put his hand on Brin's head, hoping to still the dog's trembling. "It did?"

"Oh, yes. Although I never expected more than one person at a time to break in, let alone have several people shooting at one another."

Shay had a hard time wrapping his head around it. "Were they? Or were they trying for us."

Due to that dang bonnet of hers covering up her every expression, he felt rather than saw her smile.

"Must've been at each other," she said. "Because nothing came near us."

"Yet," he said. "But, Miss January, I got a notion this little incident is gonna make a certain somebody powerful mad."

"Well," she replied as if she hadn't a care in the world, "isn't that too bad."

Shay thought maybe, yes, it was.

Just as well, he figured, when someone ran into the second of her traps. This one was not as noisy as the drum which, January explained to him later, contained mallets set in a whirring cog and mimicked gunfire. The racket had startled the intruders into firing every which way. Her next trap toppled down on unsuspecting heads. Tripped by a misplaced hand, an upright support beam popped out of place and released a shelf full of rotten hay and odds and ends of lumber and bricks on whoever stood below.

The intruders gave up after that although not

without another bullet-wasting shooting spree into the corners of the barn. But January's room wasn't in a corner. She was too wily for such a simple, obvious ploy. The room was on an outside wall, all right, but set in the middle of the barn, the entrance obscured by, among other traps, the collapsing shelf.

Shay was just as glad he was a sick man and hadn't had to contend with January's creative defenses. Moldy hay and dust made him sneeze and his nose run. And, after all, he'd found the lady a dab hand at taking care of such oddities.

Still, nobody'd ever find the like in his barn, regardless of who wanted him dead. Moldy hay where one of his horses might get at it? He guessed not.

As soon as January was certain all the men had left the barn, she followed them, a slight, barely detectable, whisper of motion. They had quite a time rounding up the fellow she'd pistol-whipped until his moans led them to him. The ruffian who'd told her he was the sheriff brought up the man's horse. Between him and January's original adversary, the young one with the bandaged hand, they managed to heft the wounded man into the saddle. Once there, he clung weakly to the horn. The sheriff led a slow cavalcade back toward town until the one who apparently gave the orders loped on ahead, leaving the others far behind in his wake.

By then it was full dark and January reported back to Shay. "They're gone." She struck a match and held it to a lamp wick, lighting her barn lantern at the same time.

Shay leaned back with a tired sigh, finally setting aside the pistol he'd been holding throughout the whole kerfuffle. "They'll be back. Them or some other of Hammel's hired men. I heard him giving orders in that high-pitched tenor of his. And he mentioned Edgar. He has a son called Edgar."

"Hammel? First name, last name or nickname?"

"Last. First name is Marvin. Don't suppose you know him. He's the one trying either to buy off or to run off ranchers along the river. Don't seem to matter much which."

"Why?"

Shay eased a small pillow behind him. "Guess he has a business proposition going that'll make him more money if others ain't involved. And whether they like it or not."

"Yes. You told me that. But why go to these lengths?"

"Ambition. Power. Who knows?" Shay hacked out a short laugh and winced. "Maybe he belongs in an insane asylum."

"I can agree with that." January picked up the

lantern by its bail and prepared to go out again, a move that roused Shay's concern.

"You best stay in. One of those yahoos might double back and lay in wait for you. No telling what they'd do if they caught you out there alone."

She had a moment of trepidation before steeling herself to ignore his advice. Oh, she knew what they'd do, all right. Or try to do. "I've got a cow to milk, Mr. Billings, if they haven't slaughtered her out of pure cussedness, as well as some chickens to feed. And horses to tend including your Hoot. The graze across his rump is healing well, by the way. It doesn't seem to bother him much."

Her comment drew a bug-eyed stare. "Graze on Hoot's rump?" Shay repeated. "What graze on Hoot's rump?"

"Didn't I tell you? I thought . . . well, that's neither here nor there. You were not the only victim in the ambush, Mr. Billings. Hoot was also bloodied though not badly." She hastened to reassure him. "A mere graze which, I repeat, is healing well."

He stared at her, seeming a little adrift.

January had a moment of self-doubt. She had told him about Hoot, hadn't she?

"Call me Shay," he said. He sounded more than a little cross.

"Shay," she repeated. "Well, Shay, I'd best get

139

to the chores before it gets any darker." This time, she set action to words, unbarring the door and slipping out. Pen, of course, went with her. That left Brin on guard although the hound appeared to be sound asleep.

The door closed behind her. At last free of an audience, she sighed and tossed back a bonnet wet with sweat to hang from the strings down her back.

Penelope ranged ahead, sometimes in, sometimes out of the light's yellow glow. The lantern swung from January's hand, gyrating with every step. Crazy shapes formed and faded. Dangerous to trust her senses, she thought, even as she kept her hand near the pistol shoved in her belt.

To her relief, she spotted the cow, both horses and her mule, black shapes almost hidden beneath the trees, safe and well. They came at her call, even Hoot, following along with the rest of his new herd. Pen met the larger critters, circling around and keeping them in a tight group for her mistress.

Exhaustion dogged January's steps by the time she finished her chores. If it hadn't been for Pen's total unconcern as they passed through the barn, she would've been frightened for almost the first time since she'd been back at the Schutt homestead.

What have I gotten myself into? The question echoed through her mind. Murderous attacks, bloodshed. Lots of bloodshed. And she didn't think it was over yet. Not until Mr. Billings—Shay—either won his battle or died. And what was anyone doing about it? That's what she wanted to know. The sheriff was one of the outlaws and the man leading the crime spree was the most powerful man in the area. And although feisty, at least from what Doc and Shay said, without a leader and someone in authority to back them up, those most directly concerned were helpless.

In fact, why is Shay a target? The question, quite suddenly, plagued her. Being on a different waterway, his land wasn't involved in the power-grab. Or was it? Her land was on the same water course as Shay's. Did that make her a target, too? A primary target, she meant, not just one from being associated with Mr. Billings.

Billings had managed to get himself back onto the cot. He lay stretched full length, his pistol beside him. He slept without movement, breathing so shallowly she thought for a moment he was dead. In a moment of near panic, she placed a trembling finger on his neck, feeling for a pulse.

His heart beat in a regular rhythm.

Pain had etched lines in his face. A nice looking face, January conceded. Pleasant and well put together, though not extraordinarily handsome. He needed a shave.

He moved a little then and she stepped back, suddenly aware she'd left her bonnet dangling. It was not for her to approve his looks. Never for her.

CHAPTER 11

Visitors the next morning disturbed Shay as, worn out from the previous night's activity, he lay dozing on the cot. He didn't know where January had gotten to although he'd been aware when she left the room. They hadn't spoken although she whispered to Brin and took the dog out, then brought her back in before leaving.

More aware than she knew, Shay sure in hell wasn't going to let on he'd glimpsed her face. Let her conceal her features within that oversized bonnet if it made her feel better. He supposed he could see her point.

Did Doc know about her face? He figured, yes. He must.

As if his wondering had conjured him, he heard Doc's voice booming through the cavernous barn as he stood just outside.

"Hallo," LeBret was shouting. "Anybody to home?"

Shay touched the ever-patient Brin's head. "Go fetch the doc, old girl. I 'spect he can't find his way. Not without getting himself conked on the head by bricks or something."

Obediently, the dog trotted off. A few minutes later, Shay heard voices.

He gave a start. Yes, more than one, and both were male.

One of them was complaining. "Damn, Doc, what kind of set-up is this?"

"Don't knock it," Doc replied. "It seems to work." And then when they stood right outside the door, "This is a right smart dog."

"Huh," the other man said.

There was a tap to announce their arrival in case Shay'd gone deaf all the sudden and hadn't heard them talking and blundering about. Surprised him that part of the roof hadn't fallen on them regardless of Brin's guidance. He had to smile at the idea of January's effective safety precautions.

Shay thought the other voice belonged to Bent Langley but, just in case, he kept his revolver in his fist, covered by the blanket. "Door's open," he said.

Doc LeBret bustled in, placing his satchel on the table beside the cot while he lit the lamp. "How you doing, son?"

Turned out Shay was right about Bent who entered right behind LeBret.

Doc brushed dust from his brown suit before bending over the cot. He studied Shay in the improved light, one of the problems with January's hidden room being that it was always dim and often downright dark. "Your color is better. Looks like the lady's chicken soup agrees with you."

"Could stand a porterhouse. A small one." Thinking of it made Shay's mouth water.

Doc laughed. "I'll let her know you're ready for a heartier diet. Where is she?"

"Don't know. Busy." Shay's lips quirked. "She's always busy."

Bent Langley stood at the end of the cot, his hat held over his heart like he'd been expecting to see a dying man. The hat had the duty of hiding the best part of Bent's worn cowhide vest. "We was worried you might die," he said. "Like Joseph."

"Feller did his best to see to it," Shay said, "but I ain't dead yet. Although I might've been if not for Miss January." His gaze moved meaningfully toward Langley. "Don't know how she's going to feel about having more visitors. Seems like this place has turned busier than the big train depot in Spokane."

Doc paused in peeking beneath Shay's bandage. "What do you mean?"

"I mean we had quite a group here last night. You might've noticed the passage is blocked."

"Yeah. I believe the dog did lead us in by a different route." Doc's eyes narrowed. "You mean January's boobytraps work?"

"Damn right, they do." Shay grinned.

"Who were the visitors?" Bent's careworn face held an eager expression like maybe he was hopeful of finding where to seek justice for his boy's murder.

Shay didn't like disappointing him but he

145

didn't feel right egging him on either. So he equivocated. "I never saw them. I heard a couple voices I'm pretty sure I recognized but I don't like to say right off in case I'm wrong. Miss January, though, she's seen 'em before. Seen 'em all. Says they were the same four as rode over to shoot up my ranch a couple days ago. Killed my chickens," he added. "All but two. Glad it wasn't my horses."

Doc LeBret fished around in his bag and brought forth something in a blue jar. Looked— and smelled—like horse liniment to Shay. "Why go over to your place at all? They knew where you were."

Bent clamped his hat back over his thinning hair. "Why'd they stop at killing just some of your chickens?"

"Oh, I figure their intention was to kill all my critters, horses, cows, chickens. But—" Shay liked telling this part. "—Miss January'd gone over to do chores and she ran 'em off."

"Ran 'em off? Four men? A woman alone?" Bent liked to strangle on his own wonder. Or maybe doubt. "How'd she do it?"

Shay shifted to a marginally more comfortable position when Doc finally quit smearing him with the salve in the blue jar which, by the way, stung like a hornet's kiss and tightened the bandages. "Miss January is a right handy woman. And that's got me worried."

146

"It does?" Bent looked bewildered.

Doc nodded. "Me, too."

"What for? Seems like a good thing to me," Bent said.

Shay sighed heavily. "Not if it gets her killed. Which it's likely to do." He struggled to work himself into a sitting position until Bent lent him a hand. Shay pressed back against the wall, ashamed of his weakness. "My fault."

"Now Billings," LeBret said, "you must know the only one to blame is the man who shot you. And you ought to know by now that January isn't putting any blame on you either."

Determined not to make any excuses, Shay said, "She don't have to. I can do that myself."

"I'd like to meet this here January female," Langley said.

The words were no more than out of his mouth than January strode in. None of the men had heard her coming, so softly did she walk. Shay couldn't see her face, of course, considering the wide-brimmed calico bonnet that threatened to overwhelm her but he knew she was blazing mad. Her whole body seemed to quiver with indignation.

"Not so sure of that," Shay sort of whispered even though he was pretty certain Bent had already forgotten what he'd just said about wanting to meet January.

"Well," she said coldly into their sudden stillness, "did you decide to hold an open house at my place and not tell me?"

Although it sounded an awful lot like recrimination, Doc LeBret was not intimidated. "Time you met one of your neighbors, January," he said. "This is Bent Langley. Bent, this is Miss January Schutt."

Bent removed his hat and nodded his head. "Miss Schutt. Pleased to meet you."

"Mr. Langley." She drew in a deep breath. "My condolences on the loss of your son."

If possible, Bent's expression became even more careworn. "Appreciate it. Just hope my other two make it out of this alive."

"I do, too. I even wish I knew what 'this' is."

Bent gaped at her. "Ain't Shay talked to you about Hammel trying to take over the whole river? And the land beside it?"

"He's told me a little. I just don't understand why this Hammel person decided to use violent means to achieve his aims. I understand he's lived here for years. Why has this turned critical just now?"

The men appeared dumbfounded by her question. Hammel's all-fired hurry hadn't struck Shay until she pointed it out but since she mentioned it, the takeovers did seem abrupt.

"I mean to say," January continued her thought, "what is the reason behind his greed? Why would he do such a thing?"

"His power plant." The explanation burst over Shay. "That's it. He's starting a power plant on the river to make electricity. A lot of electricity." Shay hadn't the least idea of how electrical power generating plants worked but he knew they required a great deal of water. Hydro something or another, they called it.

"Yeah, we know that," Bent said. "To run his new sawmill, he says."

"Sure, but how big of a power plant does he need for that? No, sir. Appears to me he has more in the works than a simple logging and sawing operation." Shay's air of confidence went more than halfway to convincing the others.

January caught on fast. "Has anyone heard of a new railroad going through? Some other big project? Why does he need so much power?"

"He didn't tell me nothing. He just went ahead and stole my water." Bent leaned against the wall, poking under his hat with a gnarled forefinger. "I don't even know why we need another sawmill. Pearson Brothers supplies all the lumber anybody needs."

"Maybe he's expecting a building boom." Doc sounded thoughtful. "I've heard rumors."

Bent scowled. "Building boom? What rumors? What're they building?"

"That I don't know."

"Apparently, that's what we need to find out," January said. "Who do you suggest we ask?"

149

"Ordinarily I'd say the mayor," Shay said. "Or the sheriff. Or the county commissioners. But . . ."

"But?"

"But the way things are, I think there's only one person we can trust."

Doc, finished with putting his salve and bandages away, flipped the latch on his medical bag closed. "Yeah? Who'd that be?"

"The governor," Shay said. "There's nobody better."

Bent was nodding. "I remember you said so before, about him being a friend of yours. Even said you'd write a letter. But how are we gonna get word to him, Shay? I don't trust our postmaster. Seems to me Eldridge is in Hammel's pocket along with half the town. Richardson was saying something about a letter going astray a few weeks ago. A stamped letter he put in the mail drop with his own hands."

"Federal offense," Doc said. "Put him in jail for that."

"Yeah, if you can prove it," Shay said. "And I wouldn't say Governor Rogers is a friend of mine exactly. More of an acquaintance. We got to know each other a little when I was working to get money to build a school in town through his Barefoot Schoolboy Act."

"You went to Olympia to meet him, as I recall," Bent said. "Pinky was real happy with the results.

Our boys got better schoolin' than I ever did. Joseph was our scholar." His voice choked at the mention of his son.

Expression sober, January broke a silence where the others found nothing to say. "Perhaps if Mr. Billings were to write a persuasive letter, Mr. Langley could carry it into Spokane to the post office there. This Hammel person can't possibly interfere with their postmaster. Can he?"

"I wouldn't think so," Doc said.

Bent's eyes lit up with a bit of hope, a bit of sparkle. "That's the ticket, Miss Schutt. Good thinking. I'll do it. I'll mail the letter from Spokane."

"Anybody got a pen and paper?" Shay asked, halfway hoping they didn't. He was afraid his hand would tremble and slop ink on the paper. Rogers was a stickler for neat penmanship, as he recalled, a quirk that dated from when he'd run a drug store in Puyallup.

He might've known January could supply the required paper, pen, and ink. Nice paper, too, he thought, rubbing it gently between his fingers when no one was looking. And a special envelope to match.

Suggestions rained down on him as to what to write. From all except January, that is. She helped in keeping it all straight and him in line so, as she said, to keep their complaint coherent. A half-hour later he was done, in more ways than

151

one. Done with the letter, done to the last of his strength, and barely hearing the woman as she hastened Doc and Bent on their way. Bent made a point of stowing the letter in the inside pocket of his cowhide vest for safekeeping.

January adjusted her bonnet to cling more tightly to her face before gathering up the extra paper, ink and pen, and envelopes and stowing them back in her trunk. They'd been set ready in case Shay mussed the original and had to copy out a new letter.

He hadn't, to his relief, since his fingers felt ready to drop off as it was. He shook his hand to start the blood flowing again.

"How soon before the governor responds?" she asked. "If he does." She punched his pillow to liven up the feathers inside and motioned for him to stretch out on the cot.

Lying back, he closed his eyes. "He always used to be Johnny-on-the-spot when it came to answering his mail. I think he'll respond." His brow crinkled. "Don't know if we'll care for what he says about the water. Unless he's changed a whole lot, I do know what he'll say about murder and a crooked sheriff. The trouble will be finding somebody able to do anything about it."

"U.S. Deputy Marshals?"

Shay heard her question but, like a light blown out, went to sleep before he could form an answer.

CHAPTER 12

No sneak attacks occurred during the next few days. January felt emboldened to get out in her garden, replanting where seeds had been ripped from the ground when the outlaws rode their horses across the soft earth, churning it and her careful planting to bits. She set both Shay's hound and her own Pen to watching for intruders and more than once she noticed one or the other sit up and scent the air.

Nothing happened though. No shots even though she made, in defiance of Shay's scolding and admonition to make herself scarce, a clear target.

All of which didn't mean she wasn't aware of eyes on her every now and then. Of an itchy feeling that made sweat break out, her muscles tense as though anticipating pain and, once, even forget to breathe until she had to gasp in air.

On Thursday, heavy black clouds rolled in over the northern mountains bringing rain with them. The horses and even the milk cow, of their own accord, took shelter in a lean-to she'd rigged up on the side of the barn. January, caught in the downpour, was forced back inside, too. With Shay. Who watched closely as she turned her back, pushed down her bonnet and dried her face and arms. Her shirt was wet across her shoulders and mud coated her boots.

Shay, not only sitting up but standing up, took the three or four steps across the room and the three or four back. Two times, three times, four times. "Dammit to hell," he said, "wish I was to home putting my mares and their foals in the barn. Don't like those young ones out in this weather."

"They'll take shelter in the grove." January swiped the towel over her hair. "I'm sure they've done it before." A sideways glance showed Shay glaring at her.

"I oughta be home looking after them," he said for maybe the fifth time.

A roll of deep, basso profundo thunder came near to shaking the building. Pen, who'd always hated storms, shook like a scared puppy and Brin howled accompaniment to the noise.

Shay winced along with the dogs. "I knew some folks," he said, "were taking a string of horses down to Fort Spokane a few years back. They got caught in a storm like this and one of the horses got hit by lightning. Set the animal on fire from the inside out, burned it up while it was still running."

He went on with a couple more gruesome details until January, made positively ill by the somber story, whirled around to face him.

"Will you kindly hush?" She set her hands on her hips. "I don't want to hear about it. It's sickening."

His dark eyes had widened, then narrowed, and he hesitated before answering. "Yes, ma'am, it is. But it's true."

"I don't care. Don't tell me. You're going to give me nightmares and I don't want them." Truth to tell, she didn't need anymore than the ones she'd lived with for most of her life.

"I don't want them either," he shot back, "but I'll have 'em if one of my animals is hit."

"What do you want me to do about it?" January, aware her voice had risen, strove to moderate her tone. "Ride over and stable them? Do you even have room for them all in the barn?" Having seen it, she knew he didn't.

A muscle flickered along his jaw. "No. 'Course I don't want you riding out. Are you crazy, woman? You might be struck yourself." Dashing a splash of moisture from his face, he gazed up toward the roof and said, "What I want is for this damn gullywasher to stop."

Indeed, as the noise of the storm grew, they smelled ozone from lightning flashing nearby. Rain drummed on the roof, starting drips here and there inside the barn including the spot almost dead-center in the room that had dropped rain on Shay. January moved to fetch a bucket and place it under the leak. The two of them clashed as Shay reached for the receptacle at the same time. Staring him in the face, January realized the sodden bonnet flopped uncomfortably down her back. And that he was seeing her full on.

A slow burn began, the heat of it traveling up her neck and into her cheeks. She whirled away. "Oh," she said.

"Who done that?"

Shay's voice was quiet but he didn't dodge from the sight of her scars. Almost as if she were one of his skittish young foals, January thought, a trace of amusement overshadowing the pain of her past and the present agony of her embarrassment and shame.

It took a moment to decide whether to answer, to find her voice. "My grandfather."

"Your grandfather?" His mouth dropped open, then closed with a click of teeth. "Old man Schutt? The feller who built this barn and then disappeared when the house burned down?"

January's stomach churned. So. He'd heard the unpleasant history surrounding the homestead. But he hadn't heard it all and she wasn't going to tell him. "Yes."

Thunder roared, Brin howled, Pen shook hard enough her toenails clattered on the plank floor, and Shay sat down on the cot like he'd slid on ice.

"You'd've been a little girl," he said when the noise outside abated. "What kind of man would do a hellish thing like that to a little girl?"

"Are you asking me?"

"Guess I don't know what I'm asking. I'm having a hard time contemplating a man taking a knife—I reckon it was a knife—to any kid let alone his own granddaughter."

"He was insane," January said.

"Belonged in an asylum then. I hear they got one over to Spokane."

"Yes. But too late for me. Too late for him as well." Stop there, she thought, say no more. She'd found Billings to be a comfortable sort of person. It would be too easy to tell him everything about the past. Better to keep the past in the past. Scars and all.

Shay opened his mouth but, to her relief, closed it again without speaking. Possibly he could read from her expression he'd best go no further. Especially when she grubbed a dry bonnet out of her trunk and jammed it on her head, effectively cutting off all discussion.

Every other week, on a Friday, January took her butter to the store in town. She earned most of her living expenses with the income derived from her butter and eggs. Demand was high for butter and she had one of the few milk cows in the area.

Hitching Molly to her small buckboard, Ernie being too cumbersome and slow for a quick trip to town, she cleared the springhouse and loaded

157

her goods. She left long before dawn in order to get there and get gone before the town woke up and hit its stride.

The rain had stopped. Although the road was a loblolly of mud and ruts, Molly was eager to stretch her legs and they made good time, reaching town just before full light. The TT Market's back door was open when January pulled up in the alley behind it. His brand new delivery truck was parked there, coated with mud past the axles. Tim Thurston, the TT of the store's name, was already busy in the store proper sweeping away dirt tracked in from yesterday's storm.

"Mr. Thurston?" January called so as not to alarm him. She'd been met with a drawn revolver once when she'd walked in unexpectedly. Apparently, he was hard of hearing and easily startled. Nowadays she was careful to give warning that she wasn't there to rob him.

"That you, Miss January?" he called back. "You bring me some of your good Guernsey cow's butter?"

"I did." She'd gotten her bonnet, which she'd had dragging at her throat from the strings, replaced on top of her head. "Twelve pounds of butter plus five dozen eggs."

"Good, good." He was already outside and going round to the back of the buggy where a wooden crate of her own construction held the eggs cushioned in little straw nests and another crate with sawdust between an inner liner and the outer shell kept the butter cool.

Thurston patted the crates. "I got a customer could use a couple of these egg crates if you're interested in building them, Miss January."

"Who?" January demanded, being particular as to who knew about her carpentry skills.

"Ollie Anderssen. He brings me eggs, too, ya know. I got customers buy up all the eggs you and his missus can produce the minute I put the sign in the store window. And your butter goes even faster. I've got orders for all of this."

"I don't know . . ." She hesitated. "I wonder if it's good business to help my competitor."

Thurston laughed, a hearty roll of sound sure to be heard up and down the quiet streets. "Well, you name a figure and I'll pass it on. If you're interested."

Due to her role of hostess to Shay Billings while he was laid up and Doctor LeBret who came to tend him, January's supply of coffee had shrunk. Likewise flour and cornmeal. She did a little shopping, enjoying the sights and smells of the store while she had it to herself. The pungent pickle barrel, the coffee beans, some early strawberries someone had brought in, glowing in a box sitting on the counter. She thought TT, a big man with plenty of belly, may have wanted those for himself but she talked him out of half.

What with the extra shopping and the discussion over crate construction, January having decided she'd build a couple egg crates for the Anderssens, she left the store later than usual when she clambered onto the buggy seat for the ride home. Taking the back street, the one that ran closest to the river, she'd almost cleared the town limits when a man stepped out in front of Molly. The horse threw back her head and came to a halt when he grabbed the reins, almost yanking them from January's hands.

She couldn't see his face as Molly's neck and shoulders kept him half-hidden. She saw he wore a badge of some sort pinned to his vest though. The town marshal?

January learned differently the second he started talking; first because she recognized his voice, second because of his threat.

"You'd be that woman squatting over at the Schutt barn," he said. "Time you was moving on. I'm giving you until tomorrow to clear out."

Bad as she hated to admit it, January's heart faltered just a little. Maybe more than a little. The surge of fear didn't stop her tongue. She thought later that perhaps it should've.

"And you'd be the rogue sheriff who is part of the gang who tried to murder Shay Billings and me the other night," she said right back.

He made a sound like a chuckle. "You'd have a helluva time getting anybody to believe that."

"Would I?" she retorted. "I doubt it'd be as hard as you think."

She reached into the buggy's footwell and grasped her .38, placing it on the seat beside her. He didn't notice as Molly, who didn't appear to care for his hand on her bridle's throat latch, kept him busy by shaking her head and trying to lunge ahead. He gave the rein a cruel jerk. Bless Molly, poor Molly.

January was closer to him than she'd been during the confrontation at Shay Billings's ranch, when she'd been too busy to get a good look at him. He stepped around her horse into plain sight and she saw that he was a hard-faced man, his complexion red, his head seeming to grow right out of his shoulders. Oddly enough, he didn't mention their first meeting. Or their second meeting, either, the one where he'd invaded her property with the intention of killing Shay and probably her, too.

He laughed, a forced laugh, his pale eyes trying to bore a hole in her. "I can guarantee if you speak out, it'll be a big mistake. Most likely your last one. And Billings, well, he ain't gonna live long enough to tell anybody his yarn. So go ahead. Make your accusations. You can't prove any of them."

Despite his threat, she squared her shoulders and put on a bold front. After all, they were within the town limits. People were beginning to move about the streets. He couldn't touch her here in the open like this. Could he?

"You think not?"

"I know not. My word—more—make that the sheriff's word against yours? I'm doing you a favor, you know, warning you to get out. Mister . . . well, my boss, he ain't much on waiting for folks taking time to see things his way. He wants it done now and my job is to see to it gets done."

"Mister? Your boss? And here I thought you worked for the people of this county. You're certainly supposed to but I assume you mean this Hammel person I've been hearing about."

"Mr. Hammel, to you. He's bought up that old Schutt place for back taxes and owns it now. His plan is to tear that ramshackle barn down."

January opened her mouth, then closed it again. Let the sheriff talk. She was learning a lot to report to Billings and Mr. Langley when she got back.

What's more, once Rhodes began talking, he just kept right on. "I've been checking," he said, grinning like he'd caught her out behind the barn with another woman's husband. "Don't anybody around here know who you are or where you came from. Won't anybody miss you when you're gone. Your only chance, missy, is to get out of the country. And make it fast. Same goes for Shay Billings. Take him along with you. Oh. And tell him to leave them horses of his right where they are. I fancy that sorrel mare that threw a palomino colt. Give 'im three years and I'll look real good settin' spur to that one."

January's lip curled in disgust even though he'd be unable to see her expression considering her bonnet's wide brim. She wasn't going to mention his mistake regarding the barn, or her, or even Shay. He'd find out. When the proper time came.

"So," she said. "You're a self-admitted horse thief as well as a murderer. What on earth were people of this county thinking when they elected you?"

"Surprising what the backing of the most important man in the country can do." The sheriff sounded proud.

"Backing?" She snorted. "You mean you've been bought and paid for."

His face suffused with red. Her accusation had struck a chord somewhere in his ego.

January's hand crept toward her pistol. "Let go of my horse," she said, her voice cool. "This conversation is finished."

"It's done when I say it's done," he said and clouted Molly hard on the neck. From his expression, he'd druther it'd been January.

A couple things happened all at once. Or maybe three or four.

One—Molly reared, almost lifting the sheriff clear off his feet.

Two—A man on horseback riding toward them

stopped, stared, then trotted forward as though to take a hand.

Three—Her dad's .38 Remington rimfire slid from the seat onto the buggy's floorboards and though she lunged for it, January's hand wrapped around the whip sitting upright in the little receptacle instead.

And four— She, who'd never dream of touching Molly with a whip, had no such compunction regarding Sheriff Elroy Rhodes. Before she even realized what she was doing, she flicked the braided elkhide whip, wrapping the lash around Rhode's arm. His gun arm as it happened. Taken very much by surprise and wincing at the pain of the lash's bite, he gasped out a curse. She jerked to loosen the lash which, January being a strong girl, caused Rhodes to not only let go of Molly but slip in the mud and tumble to the ground.

January saw her chance. "Go, Molly," she yelled and rattled the reins over Molly's back. The horse, thoroughly upset not only by the abuse but by the unaccustomed pop of a whip past her ears, took off running, traces rattling, wheels spinning for purchase in the soggy ground.

Rhodes managed to roll out of the path of the buckboard's wheels barely in time.

January didn't look back as they raced toward home. After a while, she discovered her shoulder blades were pinched tightly together and braced for a bullet in the back.

CHAPTER 13

January let Molly gallop unchecked for a half-mile or so. When the mare's gait evened out, she eased her down to a trot, then a walk. While Molly cooled, so did January. Alone on the road, she knocked back the bonnet where it flopped against her back, hanging by the strings. Sweat ran down her face from her temples, dampening her hair. The breeze, washed clean by yesterday's rain, felt good and smelled better, carrying on it the scent of pine and the wildflowers blooming along the road's verge.

She was just congratulating herself on not backing down from the crooked sheriff and on keeping certain essential things to herself when she heard a horse trotting up behind her.

Rhodes coming to take revenge?

When she retrieved her .38 this time, she made sure to keep it sitting on her lap in easy reach. She grabbed for her bonnet, stopping in mid-motion at the sudden thought that while the shadows cast by the wide brim kept her face hidden from people, it also kept them hidden from her. Wearing it, she had very little peripheral vision and wouldn't be able to see the person gaining on her. Not until it was too late.

To hades with it. Let whoever saw her think

what they wanted. Why should she care? Shay hadn't seemed sickened at the sight. Well, he had, but because of the manner of attaining the injury not because of the scars. Anyway, maybe the rider would simply pass on by without even looking at her. At least her good side was the one exposed.

January drew in a heavy breath. Controlling the reins with one hand, she kept the other on the butt of the .38.

"How do, ma'am," the rider said as he drew even with the buckboard. "Fine morning after the storm yesterday, isn't it?"

"Yes." January turned her head just far enough for a clear view of him and his horse, a creature of indiscriminate dun color. She didn't recognize the horse. Didn't recognize the man either but knew he wasn't one of the outlaw four. Not one she'd seen previously, at least. This man was youngish, about Shay's age she figured. Dark hair worn long and skin darker than most white men. Naturally darker, not sun-browned.

She blinked though noticing that his eyes, an odd amber brown, looked almost gold as the sun shone into them. His teeth were a clean white when he smiled at her. She admired a man with good teeth. January had good teeth herself, something at least her grandfather hadn't managed to spoil when he took away any pretense at beauty she might've grown up to have.

Even so, the habit of years prevented her from fully facing him.

"You're Miss January Schutt, are you not?" he said.

Startled, January pulled on the reins. "Whoa, Molly," she said. Jerking up the pistol, she pointed it at him. "How do you know my name?"

The rider reined in his horse, too, and grinned at her. "A friend of yours mighta told me."

"What friend?"

Far from flinching, the man appeared not to notice the pistol held on him. "Dr. LeBret. He said I'd better approach you carefully," he said, heavy brows arching above those odd amber eyes. "I see he wasn't wrong."

"Dr. LeBret? What's he to you? What do you want?"

"Isn't what I want. I'm here because Shay Billings wrote a letter to Governor Rogers. The letter said to contact a Doctor LeBret for more information which I did yesterday evening soon as I got here. LeBret let me know how to find you. He said you'd take me to Billings."

January's eyes narrowed. The aim of her pistol remained unwavering. "How would he know where I'd be today or, more precisely, this morning?"

The man's grin faded to wariness. He fished in a vest pocket and drew out a folded over envelope. "LeBret said you'd ask that. He told me to say that you've got a few friends in this town even if you don't realize it. The storekeeper you just consigned your butter to is one of them and evidently you have a regular delivery schedule. Today was it so LeBret sent me there. The storekeep said I'd just missed you and set me on this road."

January suspected the sequence of events had been a bit more convoluted than the simple "he told me" progression he mentioned.

She waggled the pistol at the man. "I suppose you have a name."

"I do, and a letter of introduction." Leaning from his saddle, he proffered the envelope. "My introduction is from Judge Wood. The letter to Billings is from the governor. Signed, sealed, and now delivered."

Damn. Having only two hands, January made the decision to keep Molly's reins in one while replacing the pistol in her lap with the other. She took the envelope. "Your name?" she asked insistently.

"Call me Ford." His smile came again. "Ford Tervo, at your service."

He hadn't lied. There was a seal on the envelope flap holding it closed. It appeared unsullied and seemed official. And sure enough, when she broke the seal and withdrew the contents, there was the governor's name on the outside of one document. Although how she'd know whether it was a forgery or not, January wasn't prepared to say.

With a quick glance around to see the road both behind and ahead of them empty, she unfolded and read the other page.

"This letter introduces U.S. Deputy Marshal Ford Tervo as my personal emissary," the letter said. "He carries full federal authority to investigate the crimes, both noted previously in Governor John Rankin Rogers's petition, as well as any as yet unspecified committed in the state of Washington. He is authorized to deputize men as needed to carry out his duties."

The letter's signature, a proper scrawl, appeared to be signed by a certain Federal Judge Emerson Wood.

The second letter—which January didn't feel right reading as it was addressed personally to Shay Billings, Esquire, and signed by John R. Rogers, Governor—certainly appeared as official as the state seal.

"Where's your badge?" she asked the rider, squinting at him.

He turned back a corner of his vest to reveal the marshal's service five-pointed star. Only then did January relax. Not, however, going so far as to holster her pistol.

"I'm hoping you can tell me where to find Shay Billings," Tervo said. "The judge said he'd fill me in on the situation."

January made up her mind. "I'll take you to him." She handed the letters back to him and gathered the reins into both hands. Let Tervo present his bonafides to Shay. She was out of it now.

Except she wasn't as Deputy U.S. Marshal Tervo was quick to remind her. He swung the dun in beside her as Molly picked up the pace.

"The sheriff back there that you horsewhipped, he appears a bit aggravated by the experience. If I were you, I might try to avoid him for the next few days. At least until that welt on his arm goes down." He paused thoughtfully. "And until he gets the mud washed out of his clothes."

January huffed her disgust. "I didn't horsewhip him. I simply forced him to quit manhandling my mare. But if you're scared of him, I don't need anyone riding along with me. I can tell you how to find Mr. Billings. Perhaps you'd better get along."

She didn't miss the flash of Tervo's odd amber eyes.

Voices awakened Shay. He sat up, reaching for his pistol as he braced himself against the wall. Brin had already gone to the door and was standing at attention. But not, he thought, unduly alarmed. Maybe because she recognized January's voice the same as Shay did now. But who was she talking to? Not her dog because a voice answered her. A man's voice.

He kept hold of the pistol, shoving it down beside him out of sight as the door opened.

"Don't try the maze by yourself," January was saying. "Not if you don't want a load of rocks to come down on your head."

Shay smiled when the man said fervently, "No, ma'am. I surely won't. I need all the brains I've got in this head. Some folks might say a few of them have turned to rock already."

"I'll be damned," Shay said. "Ford Tervo? Is that you?"

"In the flesh," Ford said. He was carrying an egg crate barren of eggs but piled with January's shopping. A carton of strawberries sat atop the other items. "Good to see you're alive, Billings. Judge Wood sent me, at Rogers's instigation. Hopped a train and got in last night. I hear you've gotten yourself into a whole peck of trouble."

"Seems so," Shay replied, "if you consider being shot at ambush a peck's worth. Feels more like a bushel to me. None of my doing. It ain't like I been out deliberately making enemies."

Ford grinned. "Never is."

January made a sort of snorting sound, all very ladylike as she strode over to the table and lit the lamp. "Old friends, are you?" And without waiting for a reply, "Set the box on the table, Mr. Tervo, and have a seat." She directed Ford to the only chair, stoked the stove when he'd moved out of her way, and bustled about starting a fresh pot of coffee.

Astonished, Shay noted her face was exposed at last. A shiny white scar traced out a distinct "S" on one cheek. Her grandfather had left his mark in a remarkably cruel way. Old bastard.

"Ford and I worked together for Judge Wood a few years back." Not wanting to be caught staring, Shay talked fast. He figured he'd better explain to January before her dander got agitated. "A little dust-up something like this one."

January's breath whooshed out. "Little? You call almost being murdered little? You call the Langley boy being murdered little?"

Shay sent a quick glance toward Ford. "You know I don't but I'm still here, ain't I?"

"Only because you had help before you bled out," she snapped, reaching down three cups off a shelf.

He figured he'd better quit while he was ahead—or maybe he meant before she whupped him completely.

"Well, yes, ma'am. There is that," he said meekly. He knew Ford was trying not to laugh.

The chuckle was apparent when Ford produced an envelope bearing an official seal, now broken. He thoughtfully fished out the documents and handed the governor's letter to Shay. "From Rogers," he said.

"Thanks." Shay unfolded the letter and scanned it, forehead drawing into a frown now and then as he puzzled over some of Rogers's scrawl. He took his time, reading part of the writing more than once. "Governor says here he had his secretary check the records. Nothing at the state level about either diverting the river or starting a power plant the size of the one he's got planned. Says it looks like this is a rogue operation." He read the next paragraph, then whistled. "The secretary found where an outfit named High Top Lumber Company has bought up the contract to harvest twenty thousand acres in the mountains above this valley. The secretary has connections with some of the big outfits on the other side of the state. He discovered rumors are circulating that somebody has started platting a town round and about our mountains and are demanding a rail spur into it."

"Whew!" January gasped. "That's a lot of timber. Twenty thousand acres? Are you sure?"

"According to this. All of it is state land and illegal as can be. And guess who the principal shareholder of High Top Lumber is?" He and Ford shared a look. "By gum," he said. "Hammel has more ambition than I ever gave him credit for. He's not figuring on running a sawmill. He's planning a whole lot bigger than that. For the railroad, for a new town, for the power to run the town."

Ford nodded. "And for that he needs the river." He paused. "The whole damn river."

"My little tributary as well. Every drop no matter who gets in his way."

"And your bridge is part of the road from town into the new one. There'll be more traffic than you can shake a stick at when work starts."

Ford had been busy the short time he'd been here, Shay thought. Not many men would've learned so much in only a few hours. But he had one thing wrong.

"Not my bridge." He noticed the way January, in the process of pouring coffee, dribbled liquid over the brim of one cup. He nodded toward her. "It's Miss January's."

Ford's dark eyebrows raised high over his hawk nose. "She owns this land? I'm thinking that might come as a surprise to some people."

"I'm telling you I don't own the land and I didn't build the bridge. January does and she did." Shay watched as January's eyes narrowed and a slow tide of color rose in her face. The scars from the wound her grandfather had carved there thirteen years ago stood out like a freshly painted sign. Didn't matter, he figured, or only to her. She was a pretty woman, scarred or not.

And, he noted with surprise, her eyes were not blue nor the light green like he'd expected but a shadowy dark forest green and brown mix.

Ford reached over and took the full cup from

her hand. He was grinning. "You trying to tell me a woman built a bridge? All by herself?"

"I'm right here," she said, ice in her tone. "Of course, I built the bridge. By myself. Why not?"

His amber eyes opening wide, a ploy Shay knew his friend used to entice women, Ford held up a hand as if signaling for peace. "No reason. Don't be insulted, Miss January. I just never heard of a woman building a bridge before. Takes knowing some math and some . . . some . . ."

"Basic engineering skills? Carpentry skills?" Her voice held false sweetness. "Why, yes, Mr. Tervo. It does. And it's Miss Schutt to you."

Shay burst out laughing, to January's disgust and Ford's dismay. He laughed so hard he was left gasping, nearly succeeding in busting the stitches Doc had used to sew him up. Somebody should've warned Ford that Miss January was a mite touchy.

Ford, persuaded to stay for breakfast, sat long enough to eat a half dozen of January's fried eggs, five thick strips of bacon and two slabs of toasted bread. Between bites, he outlined some ideas he'd discussed with the judge and Governor Rogers before he left the west side of the state.

"The plan is for me to join up with Hammel's outfit," he said.

January's jaw dropped and her eyes rounded. "What?"

"Yep. Go undercover. See, I can't just barrel

in and arrest people, ma'am. I need proof about the Langley boy's murder, proof about the rogue power plant and the illegal platting for a town. See, that's the bugger about this deal. Hammel's acting like he owns the twenty thousand acres but all he's got is a logging contract. The land belongs to the state of Washington. The things he's planning require licenses and fees and more cans and can't dos than you can shake a stick at. Money needs paid, plans need submitted, authorization needs received before folks start digging on public lands. And if he doesn't own the land, it's not going to go his way so he'll take it any way he can get it."

"Easier to apologize after the fact than to ask permission," Shay muttered. "Easier to pay a few folks off at the beginning, too."

"Or murder them," she said. "The strong ones. Use threats and fear against the others."

"Yep," Shay said.

Ford nodded. "You got it. And if the scoundrel has the sheriff working for him, it's all that much easier. As far as the sheriff's involvement goes, in order to take down a duly elected official, there has to be an election. A special election based on due cause. We can't just throw around accusations and expect to get him recalled." Ford took a last swallow of coffee and set his cup and plate on the too small table.

"How do you figure to infiltrate his gang?"

176

Shay asked. "Ain't he gonna be suspicious of a stranger just riding in and volunteering?"

Ford's white grin broke forth. "Nah. Not of me. See, I got an in with the sheriff this morning when I provided a sympathetic ear to his woes after Miss January took her buggy whip to him. Now he figures I'll make a fine member of his team."

"Will you quit saying that?" January had turned a hot red. "I didn't take my whip to him. I simply—"

"Yes, you did," Ford said, "and it worked out fine for our plan."

"What plan do you mean, our plan? And what are you saying, joined up?" Shay scowled.

"Just what it sounds like. The sheriff is on a hiring spree. Seems they don't have enough men to finish you and the lady off. They need a tough feller like me." Ford poked out his chest and grinned.

Unimpressed, Shay scowled. "Getting in with that bunch of ne'er-do-wells without someone to watch your back sounds mighty chancy."

Ford may have appeared nonchalant and unworried but his next words belied the attitude. "Yeah, well, Shay, you're hurt worse than we thought. Truth is, I'd been counting on you being the one to do the watchin'. Turns out we can't wait until you're well. Let this go and we'll find a group of 'investors' apt to have a foothold that's hard to break. Could be Langley will be dead by then and maybe you and Miss January as well." He nodded toward January. "Miss Schutt, that is."

"I think they've been discouraged, considering their failed attempts here," January said. "It's been four days since their last attack."

"Attack against you," Ford said.

"Now what?" Shay caught a nuance in his friend's tone that had him perking up his ears.

"Doc LeBret was called out to Langley's ranch the other morning. Seems him and his boys were hauling some hay into the barn loft when the ropes on the pulley gave way with them riding up on it. Langley himself is buggered up some with a gash in his head and a sprained ankle. One of his boys got a busted arm."

"An accident?" Shay's expression had turned hard.

"Nope." All trace of teasing and fun had gone from Ford. "Made to look like an accident, carelessness on the rancher's part, but he says not. Bentley says the rope'd been cut almost all the way through and peeled apart when it got the weight of two men on it. They fell from the top of the hay mow."

Shay twitched as if an itch he couldn't scratch had just assailed him. "No. Bent ain't careless when it comes to life and limb. Those boys of his used to use the hayloft lift as a play toy. He's sure to keep the rope in good condition even now.

Pinky, that's his wife, would make sure of that."

Eyeing January, Ford blinked. "So, you still think since Sheriff Rhodes has ignored your set-to so far, aside from your experience this morning, it means they've backed away from the fight?"

January picked up the empty dishes and carried them the two steps to a basin already filled with steaming, soapy water. "No. I guess not."

"Would be my guess they're laying off until they hatch some new plan, " Ford said. "Including hiring on more men as shown by my experience today. Maybe a real gunslinger to take you on separately. It's what I'd do if I were them. So far, they've been trying to keep this quiet. I'd guess that's not going to last much longer."

Shay nodded unwilling agreement. "After today, Rhodes is probably on the warpath and he's not a man noted for caution in what he says. January . . ."

He looked toward her only to find she was staring at Ford, her look unreadable.

Ford may have been their first visitor of the day but he wasn't their last.

On his feet at last, Shay announced to January that he was trying to regain some strength by exercising his muscles some. He'd paced a couple slow circuits around the interior of the barn before going outside to perch on the lowboy's flat bed and enjoy the sun's warmth. Brin jumped onto the lowboy beside him, curling up with her head on his thigh.

January, who hadn't the same luxury, went out to fight the interminable battle against weeds in her garden. She rolled the legs of her britches above the knee and her shirt sleeves to above her elbows in an effort to keep cool as she wielded her hoe. Her sunbonnet hung loose against her back. Sweat trickled down her face; the faded gray fabric of her shirt soon soaked through.

Although invisible herself from the road, she caught sight of a brightly-colored vehicle approaching the bridge. She paid it no mind at first. Traffic had picked up in the last few days, several stopping to examine the bridge's construction. Some of them even paid the toll.

The one that had interested her most was a horseless carriage. Shay's eyes had narrowed when, filled with excitement, she reported the sight to him, the motor car being the first she'd ever seen in motion. The only other such vehicle of her experience was T. T. Thurston's brand new Ford delivery truck and it had been motionless at the time.

The only fly in the ointment about the sighting was when Shay informed her it belonged to Marvin Hammel. What had he been doing out here where the roads were only fit for horses?

Shay suspected he'd been scouting as to whether the way was passable.

But now, Brin bayed at the front of the barn and Pen, as usual sleeping in the shade at the end of a row, stood up and stared toward the commotion.

January's hoe halted in mid-chop. "Oh, Lord, what now?" Dr. LeBret wasn't due for another visit as yet and Ford had just left. It could only, January thought, mean trouble, thankful that so far at least there'd been no gunfire.

Dropping the hoe, she skipped across rows of fledgling plants, crossing behind the barn and rounding the corner in time to see two ladies dressed in the height of fashion alight from a pretty little red-painted buggy with a fringed sunshade over the top.

One of them, a blonde who wore a green skirt and white blouse with a wide, darker green ribbon sash belt, flipped the horse's lines over the rail and called to Shay, "Good afternoon, Mr. Billings . . . Shay. Ruth and I just heard about the shooting and came to see if there's anything we can do to help. How in the world did you end up here at this falling down pile of wood scraps?"

January, mouth compressing, stepped back and spied around the corner.

Hands on hips, the blonde viewed the barn with a disparaging eye. "Can we escort you to your home where I'm sure you'd be more comfortable? This place looks like it's ready to fall down around your ears. We've brought a nice pot roast for your dinner. I see you're looking awfully thin."

January, breathing hard from her run, didn't quite know what to do. The women didn't appear dangerous. Why should she be surprised to learn Shay Billings had lady friends come to see how he was? Even though they were days late showing up with their offers of aid. Why now, after the hard nursing part of his wounding was over and just a bit more recovery to face? She peeped around the side of the barn for another look.

Dressed like ladies, fresh and clean and smiling. January wiped at her face, only noticing when it was too late that her hands were not only rough but filthy from digging out weeds inaccessible to the hoe.

The brown-haired woman looked almost exactly like the other except for the difference in their hair and the color of her skirt and belt sash. This one wore muted blue plaid. She'd paused to retrieve a basket from the back seat of the buggy and wasn't far behind the blonde.

"And pie," she said. "I baked you an apple pie. Fresh out of the oven only two hours ago and still warm. Becca, you haven't allowed Shay to get a word in edgewise." She reached out to shake his hand. "How you doing? Feeling all right? You do look a bit peaked."

Shay, closing his mouth with a snap, abandoned his seat on the lowboy and brushed dust from the seat of his pants. "Miss Ruth, Miss Rebecca. How did you hear about me being shot? How did you know where I was?"

The women shared a glance and the brown-haired one raised a brow. She wore a broad-brimmed straw hat, one with a veil and a cluster of fruit and feathers stuck to one side of the crown. "Sheriff Rhodes spoke to you, didn't he, Becca?"

"Why, yes, you know he did. I told you all about it." The blonde turned to Shay. "He said you were holed up in this awful old barn and in pretty bad shape. He said there's some strange wild woman out here with you and he's afraid she's holding you captive."

"That's if she didn't shoot you herself," the brown-haired one said. "He told Becca he thought it a possibility since you didn't see who did it."

"He told you all that?" Shay said.

Ruth may have heard some nuance in his tone because she said slowly, "Isn't that right?"

"About fifty-fifty," he said after a moment of thought.

Rebecca huffed. "Are you saying the sheriff is wrong?"

"Which fifty is right and which is wrong?" Ruth asked.

Shay's attention drifted until he focused on the corner of the barn concealing January. "He's right about me being holed up in this here barn. And I was in pretty bad shape after getting ambushed. I'm better now." A grin quirked. "But nobody is holding me captive, as you can plainly see. I'd be interested to hear why Rhodes don't think I know who done it. He ain't been here to ask me any questions."

Ruth stared at him. The blonde flounced.

"There is no wild woman either, although me and Hoot and ol' Brin," he patted the hound's head, "got us an angel lady." He smiled and, even from a distance, January thought she saw a tinge of deviltry in it. "Miss January," he called, "you come on out here and meet a couple of your neighbors."

Right about then, given four cents, January would've clobbered him one. Anybody, she thought fiercely, ought to know a woman didn't want to meet people—especially two strange, fresh and pretty women cooing softly to a man—when she was hot, dirty and smelling of hard-earned sweat. But, by golly, she took umbrage at that wild-woman comment.

Taking a deep breath, she set herself and emerged from her hiding place. It wasn't far to where the three stood and she was the same as there before she remembered her bonnet. Too late now. Her scarred cheek exposed, she lifted her chin, narrowed her eyes, and held out her hand to Ruth who was nearest.

"How do you do," she said, prim as any antiquated spinster. "I'm Miss January Schutt, owner of this awful old barn."

Ruth shook with a firm grip. "Ruth Inman, pleased to meet you. This is my sister, Rebecca."

Someone had mentioned the Inman sisters, January remembered. Most probably Bent Langley. She also remembered he'd said they were both looking for husbands and Shay Billings headed up their list.

Rebecca had a softer, briefer touch. "Charmed, I'm sure."

January was quite certain she wasn't charmed at all. "Please excuse my dirt," she said. "I've been hoeing the garden. Trying to keep ahead of the weeds is a full-time job."

Small talk about gardens didn't go far. Ruth, at least, had her eye on the details. She turned back to Shay as if January didn't count for much. "Did you see who shot you?" she demanded of him. "If so, why isn't Rhodes doing anything about it?"

"Oh, hush, Ruth," her sister said. "I'm sure Elroy just . . . just . . ." She faltered to a stop before saying, "Why would anyone want to shoot you? That's what I want to know."

"Have you been going around making enemies?" Ruth chimed in.

Shay looked a little spooked but he wasn't about to let the women get the upper hand. "Guess you'd have to ask Rhodes why he isn't doing anything. Did I see who shot me? No. That's the point of being dry-gulched, ladies. The coward hides out where he can't be seen and shoots from cover."

"Well then," Becca said, "so you didn't see who shot you."

Easing himself back onto the lowboy, Shay shook his head. "Not me, but Miss January did."

Two sets of blue eyes swiveled to study January. "Well?" Ruth said. "Who did it?"

January hated them for staring at her. For seeing the scar. The grotesque "S" on her cheek, permanently standing out like a sign painted on a storefront. Look here, it seemed to say.

She swallowed and found her voice. "I don't know his name but I know a lot about him. Shay knew at once when I told him."

The two turned as one to face Shay. "Who?" Ruth demanded but Shay shook his head.

"Miss January will tell you. See if you can figure it out." With an apologetic grin, he nodded encouragement to her.

"It happened the afternoon of the Bentley boy's funeral," January said. "I was hauling rocks out of the pasture when I noticed a man on a horse in the underbrush down by the bridge. He just sat there as if he was hiding out waiting for someone. But he wasn't doing anything wrong so I forgot about him and went back to work. Before long, I spotted Mr. Billings on his gray horse cross the bridge, headed for his home. A few minutes after that, when he passed out of sight over the hill, the man I'd seen before rode out of the brush and followed him."

Both women stared at her.

"Yes?" Ruth said. "Then what?"

"I heard a gunshot. And then a second one." January didn't like reliving that moment. "Next thing I knew, the horse and rider who'd followed Shay blasted over the hilltop like they'd been shot from a cannon, the rider whipping the horse with his reins. I started for the bridge, thinking to ask what had happened but he was going too fast. That's when Hoot came running, too, without Mr. Billings on board. I guess he was following the other horse. I saw blood on the saddle and blood on Hoot's rump where he'd been grazed by a bullet. Not that I knew it was a bullet at the time although I had a pretty good guess. So I caught him up and rode him back to look for Mr. Billings who I found lying in the road, unconscious and bleeding badly."

The Inman sisters took a few moments to coo over Shay again. To January's amusement, he turned a bright red. The women weren't diverted for long.

"That tells us what happened," Ruth said. "Quite self-evident, I'd say. But you're not saying who the man was . . . is."

"Yes," Becca chimed in. "Who was it? Just tell us."

Shay shook his head. "Describe him, Miss January. I want them to figure it out."

She nodded. "First, the horse. It's quite distinctive. A pinto, a medicine-hat pinto, white with black patches including a heart-shaped one on the chest. A fine looking animal."

The women reacted, the blonde with a whispered, "No. Why, that sounds like—"

She hadn't even told Shay the next detail so he was as surprised as the others when she mentioned the saddle with a red-dyed seat and stirrup cups with an E.H. emblazoned on them. That part she'd seen when he shot the chickens and knew him for the same man. What she didn't say was that the initials reminded her of the scar on her own cheek, a detail she wasn't likely to miss.

"Lest you think I'm accusing this man, not as an eyewitness but as someone making an educated guess, that isn't the only time I've met him. Two nights later, he entered the barn with the intention of murdering Mr. Billings. And me, I suppose. If it weren't for my good dog, he might've succeeded."

Oohs and ah recorded the women's response.

"What happened?" Rebecca gasped out.

"I have safety features in place. He ran into a couple of them. But the main thing, for your information, is that time I saw the man's face when he lit a match. He's young, I'd say not yet twenty. He wears his hair long and it's every bit as blond as yours, Miss Inman." January's gaze found Rebecca and lingered a moment.

"He's thin and his front teeth stick out. So do his ears, so much they poke through the hair. At this point, he wears a bandage on his left hand, his gun hand."

Ruth shared a long look with her sister. "Does he? Why?"

"My dog bit him when the fellow tried to shoot her." January smiled crookedly. "Bit him hard enough he dropped the pistol he was holding. He fell over a wagon tongue and, going by the yells, must've banged himself up. It was enough to discourage him and he ran, leaving his pistol behind. I have it and can show it to you if you'd like. You'll find it quite unique, certainly not a regular working man's possession."

Ruth's mouth puckered. "Let me guess. A long-barrel Colt with pearl grips."

Shay nodded wryly.

"You know him?" January looked from one woman to the other.

"Oh, yes. You've perfectly described young

Edgar Hammel. His daddy gave him that pistol on his sixteenth birthday. He's a wild one, for sure." There was nothing girlish about Rebecca now. "Gunning Shay down sounds exactly like something he'd do. Remember, Ruth, when he took that same gun and shot one of Mr. Rotchford's prize sheep dogs? Right in front of the whole town."

"I remember," Ruth said. "And his father laughed."

"And neither Marshal Metzger nor Sheriff Rhodes did a thing to punish him," Rebecca finished, shaking her head sorrowfully. "I've always thought the less of them for that."

"You have? Then why are you always defending the sheriff?" Ruth demanded.

The Inman ladies were still gently quarreling when they departed, leaving an exhausted Shay to January's not-so-tender ministrations.

CHAPTER 14

January, arms akimbo, head cocked and lips compressed, stood watching as Shay pulled on his boots. Unsurprised, she noted he was sweating profusely by the time he succeeded.

"You're not well enough," she insisted. "Look at you. You're weak as . . . as a worm."

Shay scowled at her. "The hell," he said, resting on the edge of the cot before attempting to rise to his feet. He swiped at a drip of sweat running from temple to chin. "Miss January, you know as well as I do it's past time I left here. I don't know what's happening with my horses or even if the house is still standing."

"It's standing," she said. "At least it was day before yesterday when I went over to check."

He didn't appear assured. "Or if my two chickens are still alive."

"They are," she said, "as long as a coyote hasn't forced its way into the coop."

"And me or Brin not there to defend them." Jamming his hat onto his head, Shay got his feet under his center of gravity and pushed up. Successfully, as it happened, though not effortlessly. "Did you bring Hoot in from the pasture like I asked you?"

"Yes." She'd turned away so she wouldn't have to watch his pathetic struggle. "But I'm not going to saddle him for you. You need to prove to me you can do it yourself. You'd better be able to unsaddle him when you get home, too—if you make it there in one piece."

"I'll make it."

January thought he most probably would. Mr. Shay Billings was a determined sort of man and he'd seen ten days in her care. Long enough for his wounds to close so she didn't need to worry her patient would bleed to death. Overwork his heart maybe and suddenly keel over she considered a different possibility.

Another possibility, of course, included somebody dry-gulching him again on his way home. She'd felt eyes on her more than once in the last few days, enough to put a sharp edge on her fraught nerves. It seemed certain that besides Sheriff Rhodes, Marvin Hammel and his group of thugs were keeping close tabs on her and Billings. The only question was when they'd choose to make their next move. It would be best if they didn't know Shay had left for his own place. Not right off, anyway.

Which made this a pretty good day for him to leave. There'd been no eyes today. So far.

She had to lead the way out of the room since Billings wasn't quite up to finding his own way past her traps. They stopped at an open space, an area where he'd had a line of sight to watch her work on a table in progress.

"One more coat of varnish and it'll be done." She ran a forefinger over the smooth top, pretending not to notice as Shay stopped for a moment, struggling with his breathing. The shot had nicked his lung which was still leaking air and giving him fits.

"It's a pretty piece of work," he said when he could. He reached to touch the surface, drawing back at the last moment. "You going to sell it?"

"No. It's for me. For my house, when I finally have enough money to get it built." She paused. "If ever."

She guided him outside through the entrance obscured by the collapsed roof and on to the corral where Hoot was already bridled, the reins flipped around an iron ring set through an upright post.

Hoot nickered and tossed his head as if saying "Howdy."

"He's glad to see you," January said, smiling at Shay.

"Yeah. Me, too." Shay's first action, aside from giving the horse a friendly pat and speaking to him, was to examine the bullet graze on his rump. The area, healed now, still lacked hair and possibly always would.

"He's all right," January said. "I told you so."

"Yes, ma'am. I just like to see for myself."

January huffed.

She'd hung Shay's saddle over the fence rail

earlier and watched now as he examined the blanket for burrs or the like. She could've told him there were none, concluding with an inward sigh that he still would've looked for himself.

He managed the blanket fine. The saddle, though a regular stockman's variety, proved a more awkward burden in his weakened state. Eventually, the horse was saddled and cinched.

"I said I'd be fine," he told her, leaning against Hoot who shifted his weight to accommodate him. "And I am."

"Fine?" She eyed him, brow arched. "Funny. You don't look fine to me. You're as pale as Bossy's cream and sweating rivers."

It was true, too; his skin pasty, his shirt turned dark with moisture. He turned to mount the horse, stepping in close and hanging on to the saddle with one hand, lifting and guiding his foot into the stirrup with the other.

It didn't work.

After several seconds, January moved up and formed a bridge with her hands. "C'mon. I'll give you a boost."

The mounting process accomplished, Shay settled into the saddle and looked down at her. "I thank you for saving my life, Miss January. And for looking after Hoot and riding over to my place, and for taking care of ole Brin. We owe you."

January shook her head. "No debt. I'm glad

I was here and able to help." She shook her forefinger at him. "You lie low and rest when you get home. Don't go undoing my work."

"No, ma'am." He grinned down at her and clucked at Hoot who immediately spun and stepped forward. But Shay drew him in and turned back to her. "If they come after you, Miss January, you break away and come on over to my place as fast as that Molly horse of yours can run. We'll chase them off in short order, just like we did before."

He seemed to have forgotten it was her booby traps in her barn that had turned the trick. Even so, she nodded and said, "Same to you. And if you see Mr. Tervo, if he's even still alive, tell him to drop by here, too. I want . . . no, I need to know if he's made any progress. Most particularly what the sheriff has planned for us."

"I'll tell him," Shay promised, already some distance away. "But I figure we know what Rhodes has planned. I doubt you'll like what Ford has to say."

"No. I probably won't," she whispered so only Pen could hear.

Shay's whistle pierced the air and Brin, who'd been sitting on her haunches looking first at him and Hoot then back at January and Pen, jumped up and bounded after him.

He waved as they crossed her bridge. No toll, which made her smile. A smile that faded as Pen, sitting beside her, gave out a lonesome-sounding moan.

January scratched behind the dog's ear. "I know," she said. "Already feels empty, doesn't it? Sort of scary empty, like we've been abandoned. Like somebody could sneak up on us when we're not looking. We need to stay alert, Pen."

Pen's tail beat a short tattoo against January's legs.

January scanned the hills around the homestead, searched the trees over by the river crossing and around the edge of her pasture. She saw nothing. Nothing alarming anyway. It struck her as odd. Those men hadn't scrupled at murder. Not of a fifteen-year-old boy and not an attempt on Shay Billings who was simply going about his business.

They hadn't been squeamish about attacking her either and she didn't suppose she was any safer than Shay. After all, she'd seen them. She knew who they were. Were they really so confident they had the upper hand that they felt she was no longer a threat?

Unlikely. She knew that. She'd seen hate in Sheriff Rhodes's eyes. He'd never let their run-in pass. If he'd won, maybe, but not when she'd gotten the upper hand. What was he waiting for?

A last examination of the countryside showed birds in flight on their usual paths. Bugs hummed and chittered. A chipmunk ran past her, undisturbed by her presence. Smoke from her morning fire still rose from the pipe on the barn's roof, scenting the air. All was well.

Except, where was Ford Tervo? Why hadn't he been around to see Shay? Had he, with his cocky grin and easy ways, met murder when he joined up with Rhodes and Hammel's outlaws?

These questions and more plagued January as she found her hoe and trudged out to the garden. Weeds, mainly ignored because of the company she'd entertained during the last week or so, had been making inroads into her tidy rows. Time to root them out. And after that came the final coat of varnish on her table.

She set to chopping the weeds, wishing they were Sheriff Rhodes and his ruffians.

Shay sagged in his saddle like a sack of lumpy onions by the time he reached the ranch yard. The sorrel mare, Hoot's dam and the first of Shay's breeding stock, hung her head over the corral fence to gape at him. She nickered softly and nosed the colt, nearly Hoot's twin, that stood at her side twitching his bushy tail.

"Been missing me?" Shay called to her, surprised to find his voice weak.

Hanging onto the horn, he rode into the barn before lowering himself to the ground. If he tugged off the saddle and bridle, he could just leave them lay in the straw out of the weather and turn Hoot loose. He figured it was the best he could do right now. At the last second, he pulled his carbine from the scabbard and took it with him.

Brin followed Shay to the house, staying close to his side. They climbed onto the porch where the dog nosed her empty water dish, now filled with a generous sprinkling of dust.

"Sorry, old girl," he said. "Come on in. I'll pump you some fresh in the kitchen." Even then, he took the time to hang onto a porch pillar and gaze around. His two big white chickens, as January had said, were inside the fenced enclosure pecking energetically at the ground. Off in the distance, down by the rushing creek, he saw at least part of his small herd of cattle taking their ease amongst the trees. A couple of his horses, sensing activity at the house, were headed his way, each of them no doubt looking for a handful of oats. They were followed by two sorrels. The sight brought a smile to his face, the first in days.

Shay spotted the note on his table as he lurched to the sink with the intention of pumping Brin's water. Holding his curiosity at bay, he filled the dog's dish and splashed some water into a glass for himself. It was good water. Cold from the spring above the house and one of the reasons he'd chosen this site to build on. Collapsing onto a chair, he unfolded the paper.

Although the note bore no signature, he knew

from the bold hand that Ford had written it.

"I'm in," he read. "You and the lady take care. He isn't happy with the way things are going, what with you and that rancher holding firm. I'll try to let you know any plans ahead of time but don't count on it."

Shay figured Ford thought he was being cagey by not spelling things out but it seemed plain enough to him. What's more, he had no doubt Rhodes wouldn't be fooled either had he chanced to read the missive.

He didn't make it as far as the bedroom but fell asleep where he sat, slumped over the table with his head on his arms, the note still between his fingers. Two hours later, stiff and in pain but feeling stronger, he awoke to the sound of horses in the yard. Brin was standing by the door, the ridge of hair along her spine standing on end, a low growl curling in her throat.

"Hush now," Shay whispered, hoping she wouldn't start baying. He lurched to his feet, thankful for the holstered .44 revolver hanging from a peg beside the door and that he had his carbine handy. "Let's see who it is before you start making a racket."

With Brin following on his heels, he picked up the carbine and padded over to the kitchen window where, staying to the side where he couldn't be spotted through the glass, he peered out-side.

There were two of them. Two he could see anyhow.

First, Edgar Hammel, the young feller who'd already done his best to kill him. The other he recognized from January's description as one of the men who'd participated in the slaughter of his chickens and in the attack at her barn.

Shay's eyes narrowed. Bastards back to finish the job from the look of things, their intention this time to burn him out. Each man carried a torch that appeared to have been dipped in tar.

Well, by God, they were in for a surprise. They clearly weren't expecting him to be holed up in the house and were not only taking their time lighting their torches but talking openly in loud voices. While Shay was inclined toward blowing them both out of the saddle without warning, he held fire. Maybe if he listened a while, he'd learn their plans by hearing their talk. After all, knowledge was power. He'd read that somewhere once.

"Which should we do first, Eddie?" the second man called over to his partner. "Reckon we ought to rope that horse Elroy wanted and bring'er back to your dad's place? Best to get'er caught so's the fire don't spook 'er."

Edgar Hammel rooted about in his shirt pocket, eventually coming up with a match. "Suck'n up to ol' Elroy, Billy?" He laughed. "Go ahead. I don't need no help tossing a brand through the winder of this crummy house."

Billy, in the process of freeing up his rope, scowled at Edgar. "Reckon I don't need help roping a horse either. Kinda seems a shame to burn the house down though. It's a nice house."

Damn right it is and it's mine and I ain't letting any sonuvabitch burn it down over my head. Raising his carbine, Shay levered a cartridge into the chamber.

Sensing trouble, Brin looked up at him.

"Yep, old girl, looks like we're gonna do us a little hunting," he told her. "Like shooting sitting ducks."

Brin's tail wagged.

But then Shay couldn't bring himself to pull the trigger. Sitting ducks. Yeah, but he'd never been much of one to hunt in that fashion. He preferred his prey on the fly. Give'em a chance. Granted, these here yahoos weren't ducks but they made a bigger target. Easier to hit. And when you came right down to it, he didn't like the idea of shooting anything from ambush. It made him no better than they were.

Cursing himself for a fool, Shay sucked in a breath, steadied himself, then pushed open the window in hopes it wouldn't get shattered by gunfire. The outlaws were so busy yapping back and forth, they didn't notice the rough slide of the window going up.

"You out there," Shay shouted, his voice strong.

"Throw down them torches and put your hands up."

He knew they wouldn't do it. Which was fine with him except the Hammel kid had faster reflexes than he'd expected. Edgar spurred his horse, causing it to jump sideways. At the same time, he drew his pistol and snapped off a shot. Ill-aimed as it happened, though passing squarely through the open window to plow into the wall in back of Shay.

Shay ducked to the other side of the window, keeping Edgar in sight. And his aim turned out better than the kid's. He squeezed off his shot. Edgar grabbed at his neck as a stream of red spurted out and gushed over his chest.

Instantly, Shay shifted the barrel of his carbine toward Billy and fired.

"Missed." Maybe he spoke to Brin, who was whining and digging frantically at the door, or maybe just to himself.

The young outlaw had set spurs to his horse and was in retreat by the time Shay levered in another shell, slowing some as he turned the corner at the side of the house. Billy turned in his saddle, lifting his rifle and letting fly in Shay's direction before setting out again. Shay didn't know where the bullet went. Nowhere near him, he thought, firing again after the fleeing man. He wasn't trying real hard to hit him for fear of shooting the horse instead.

With three shots, Shay was done, exhausted by the effort. Brin pressed against his side and Shay wondered if her ears hurt as badly as his. Shooting inside a closed-up house wasn't to be recommended.

But exhausted or not, with his ears pulsing painfully and Edgar down in the dusty yard flopping around like one of Shay's slaughtered White Langshan chickens with its head off, he had to take some action.

Grunting, he lowered his carbine. "C'mon, Brin," he said, gesturing her outside with him. Shay was careful to spot the dust trail left by Billy's horse, making sure the outlaw hadn't doubled back, before he went over to where young Hammel sprawled in the dirt.

Edgar's pistol lay beyond him but Shay gave it an extra kick just to make sure he couldn't reach it. No need, he saw then. Edgar's hands were at his throat trying to hold back the blood. Not having much luck at it either. Tears streamed from his eyes and he was bawling like a baby.

Shay stood over him and watched the spurt of blood slow and the kid's threshing movements go still.

After a while, he prodded Edgar in the belly with the carbine's barrel.

Edgar didn't move.

"Well, hell. Now what should I do with you?" Shay said but he was talking to a dead man.

CHAPTER 15

January straightened and stretched her aching back, leaning on her hoe. As had become a habit, she scanned the hills overlooking the homestead for unexpected motion. Checked the sky for precipitous flights of birds, listened for insects gone suddenly silent. She'd been doing that a lot of late, especially as traffic picked up on the road going past her barn once it became known the bridge had been repaired. There'd been five or six travelers today since Shay had left, at least four of whom dropped coins into the toll box. Each traveler had taken the road headed toward one of the little mining towns that'd sprung up in the mountains.

Or perhaps the one Marvin Hammel and Sheriff Rhodes intended to create and supply with electricity and lumber, she thought sourly.

None of the riders had stopped or even glanced toward the barn. Apparently. Just as apparently, nothing stirred in the trees at the edge of the field where she'd been working. Or even beyond the garden in the pasture where Molly, Ernie, and the cow grazed, gradually working their way toward the barn as the afternoon drew on. A glance showed Pen lying on the grass at the end of a bean row, head on her paws, peacefully watching January work.

Whooshing out a breath, January started to relax until a moving object on the road across the river caught her attention. Still too far away to positively identify, she squinted, wishing she possessed a pair of field glasses. The critter, which she soon made out to be a riderless horse, was ambling slowly her way.

Not, she saw, with a relieved quiver inside, a gray horse. Not Hoot. This one was dark, a brown or a bay.

As it came closer, she saw it bore a saddle and the bridle's reins were trailing.

Pen had noticed the animal now, too. Rising, the dog padded over to January and looked up at her as if asking a question.

"No, indeed. That horse didn't saddle itself to go for a walk," January said, giving Pen's ears a scratch. Her mouth had gone dry. This was a scene entirely too reminiscent of when she'd found Hoot. And then Shay, nearly dead.

Except, she reminded herself, this wasn't Hoot. Or Shay.

Pen leaned into the caress and wagged her tail.

They watched a few minutes longer. Twice the horse stepped on the end of the reins, causing its head to jerk and its feet to stumble.

January sighed. "I suppose we'd better do something about that, hadn't we?" she asked the dog.

Pen's tail whipped harder which January took for agreement.

It took January only a few moments to catch Molly and throw the saddle on her. By the time she and Pen had crossed the bridge, the horse was close enough for her to see a dark stain on the saddle and splashed down its side.

"Not again." The words came out on a gasp. Dread laid a leaden hand on her.

"Whoa, there," January said when Molly drew even with the other horse. Obedient to the command, the horse stopped. January reached down and grabbed the trailing reins while Pen went around and sniffed. The dog's hackles rose at the scent of blood, a reaction January felt as well.

"Where'd you come from, hey?"

The horse tossed its head at the sound of her voice, seeming to take issue when January said, "We'll have to backtrack." And when the horse refused at first to budge, "I don't blame you. I'd druther not myself."

But duty called. And dread. And that all-consuming out-and-out fear. Sure of where the backtracking would take her, she tugged on the reins and urged the horse into motion.

"If I'm wrong," she announced, maybe to the horse, maybe to her dog, "Shay still needs to know."

But she wasn't wrong.

A mile her side of the cut-off to Shay's ranch,

she found the body of a man. His head pointed toward the main road as though he'd been riding away from the ranch. He lay on his belly, crumpled in the dirt road with a tell-tale trail of dried blood behind him. All January had to do was follow it and she'd find out where he'd come from.

Dismounting, she tethered Molly and the riderless horse to a branch of a nearby fir. Reluctant as she may be, she had to find out for sure if the man was dead. And see if she could identify him, an unlikely situation considering her lonely existence and lack of acquaintance with her neighbors.

Pen paced forward with her, moaning low as she sensed death and January's distress. Distress that increased when January realized she recognized the man after all, although she couldn't put a name to him. The man, decidedly dead, was one of the gang who'd shot Shay's chickens. Also the one she'd thumped over the head on the day the outlaws had attacked her barn with the intention of killing Shay. He'd taken a bullet that, if it hadn't hit a rib which apparently, judging by the damage, caused it to ricochet around in his body, would probably have been only a minor wound.

"Damn," she whispered. She looked at Pen. "You know him, too, don't you? Worse, where we find one of these murderers, I expect we find at least one other. So where is he?"

Pen cocked her massive head to one side.

"And where is Shay?" January's voice trembled.

She didn't try to do anything with the body, leaving it just as she'd found it. Mounting Molly and leading the other horse, she went on. The blood trail led straight to the gate leading to Shay's ranch.

At first glance, all appeared well. No pitched gun battles in progress to break the silence, at least.

Stopping on the slight rise above his place, she had a good view. Shay's horses grazed undisturbed in the pasture. She spotted Hoot in the corral, his saddle, to her relief, removed so she knew Shay had made it home in one piece.

It was the pinto with the heart-shaped patch standing hipshot outside the house that caused her heart to flutter. There was no sign of the pinto's rider or of Shay. And no Brin come to investigate the new arrivals.

Pulling the rifle from the scabbard on the dead outlaw's saddle, January levered a cartridge into the chamber just in case.

"C'mon, Molly." She nudged the horse in the ribs. The bay, his neck stretched with his reluctance, followed and with Pen panting alongside, they made their way down to the yard where the pinto nickered a greeting.

"Mr. Billings?" January called the name softly. Truth be known, barely above a whisper what with her every nerve on alert. She thought she heard a woof which caused her to startle but saw no sign of Brin. Pen, however, pricked her ears and trotted over to the other side of the porch; the side nearest the chicken coop where the two live chickens were getting a last scratch in the dirt before dark and a peck at whatever they stirred to the surface.

Then Pen let out another of those pained moans she was in the habit of uttering when something didn't suit her and January's heart about stopped. One of the chickens clucked a questioning note.

"Oh, God. Shay?"

It took everything she had for January to slide from the saddle and step around the porch to the other side, the rifle she carried at the ready.

She found two bodies sprawled on the ground. The first lay face up in a mess of drying blood, his arms flung wide, his eyes glazed in death. The other was in the shade of one of the young trees planted alongside the house. The second man lay on his side, head pillowed on an arm with his eyes closed. Brin lay on her belly beside this one, her gray muzzle resting on his arm. A carbine lay near to hand.

"Shay?" January started toward him.

He reached for the carbine even as his eyes fluttered open, curbing the motion in mid-reach as recognition dawned. "How do, Miss January. How'd you know I needed help?" He paused.

"Again." He sounded strong if a bit weary.

"Have you been shot?" She had one of those weighted pauses, too, as she stopped beside the dead man. Yes. Definitely dead. Too much blood had spilled for any other outcome. "Again?"

"Shot? No, ma'am. Though it ain't for lack of trying." He glanced around, frowning as his gaze landed first on the dead man, then at the hitching rail where Molly and the bay stood. He sat up slowly and with some effort, bracing his back against the tree.

"Just tuckered," he said. "I started in to drag this feller away. Didn't want him stinking up my porch. His partner got away. Except—" His frown grew fierce. "Where'd you get that horse?"

"He was wandering loose across the river from my place. Riderless, with blood on his saddle. Just like Hoot the day you were shot."

The puzzled expression that spread across his face was something to see. Puzzled? January snorted. Dumbfounded, more like.

"Blood on his saddle? You mean to say I hit him?" he said. "The bay's rider? Or did somebody else? You?"

"Well, someone did but not me. He's certainly dead, lying on your property just over the hill."

"I'll be da . . . danged." Shay's lip went up in a scornful curl. "Me then, I reckon. What happened was the eggsucking son-of-a-gun hightailed it out of here when the bullets started flying. Which was fine with me. I fired off a shot when he was almost over the hill and figured to miss. Hell, I wasn't even aiming at him. He shot at me with his handgun. I just wanted him to keep on going and not come back." He rubbed his chin. "Which he did. Keep going, I mean."

"And he won't be coming back," January said dryly.

Shay went quiet for a moment. A pensive kind of quiet, she thought.

"Well," he said after a while, "I ain't sorry." Grabbing a low-hanging branch and using his carbine for a brace, he pulled himself up.

January, being a practical woman, tamped down a surge of revulsion regarding the situation. Death, murder, unmitigated greed. Sometimes it seemed that's all she'd ever in her whole life known.

She looked down, nudged the dead man lying at her feet and, disgusted, shook her head. "One outlaw fewer to worry about. Or make that two outlaws fewer. And I'm not sorry either."

But she was. A little. Sorry about a situation she wanted no part of.

Shay shook his head. "Except this outlaw happens to be Marvin Hammel's son, his only son, and he ain't going to take it well."

The long afternoon had turned to evening by this time. Shay's two remaining chickens climbed their ladder to the roost to settle in for the night.

His horses ambled back to the pasture while Hoot stood hipshot in the corral, a wisp of hay hanging from his mouth. Molly and the two horses that'd belonged to the outlaws switched their tails at flies as they waited for someone to care for them. The evening supply of biting insects gathered around the dead outlaw, leaving the living alone for a change.

"What are we going to do with the bodies?" January had just passed the question to Shay when the sound of a horse making haste toward them reached her ears. Brin and Pen both stood up and faced the road.

Shay, moving faster than she'd ever seen him, grabbed January's arm and pulled her with him around the corner of the house. Then he sort of tucked her in behind him.

That particular corner was getting a lot of use it had never been intended for, she thought.

"Who is it?" she whispered.

"Don't know yet. It ain't like I'm expecting company."

The horse slowed, then stopped. January tried to see around Shay's shoulders before peeking under his arm. He settled the arm around her, most likely because he needed someone to lean on as he craned his neck to see the rider.

"Hello the house," a man called out. "Anyone here?" Whoever it was paused a beat. "Anyone alive?"

CHAPTER 16

Shay gave a little start and gusted out a breath it seemed he'd been holding endless minutes instead of a few seconds. "Ford? Is that you?" he called out. Beneath his encircling arm, he felt January's shoulders go slack as her pent-up breath released in tandem with his own. "Sounds like Ford found the other feller, too," he said to her.

"It's me, all right." Ford swung down from his horse, leaving it ground-hitched beside the others at the rail. He glanced over at the dead man, mouth twisting under his full mustache. "Huh. Eddie Hammel. Wondered where he'd got to today. Him and Billy both." He eyed Shay with a stern look.

Shay stepped away from January and toward Tervo. "Now you know."

"Now I do. I expect you're aware this isn't going to sit well."

"Yeah, but I didn't much care for the alternative either."

"No. I expect not." Ford grinned, tilting his head in an attempt to see around Shay. "How do you do, Miss January. So you're here, too."

She nodded coolly. "As you see. I'm beginning to think rounding up runaway horses and

213

searching out their disabled or dead owners is my lot in life."

Shay couldn't help it. He grinned at Ford's blank look. "First me, when Eddie gunned me down, then that Billy feller today. Seems I hit him with a stray shot."

One of Ford's eyebrows lifted. "A stray shot? Like an accident?"

"Yeah."

"I'll put that in my report to the judge."

"Do you have to tell the judge about this?" Shay surveyed Edgar's body, looking down with a wry expression on his face. January hung back when Ford joined him.

"Yep. Ah, what were you planning to do with the corpse?" Ford pointed to the short drag marks. "Bury him?"

"Thought about it. Started to before I came over all weak. Then I figured Elroy'd just come out here flaunting his badge and accusing me of murder anyway so I had it in mind to dump him in the river upstream of Hammel's dam. Was thinking on how I could get him back up on his horse and went to sleep standing up. My thought was that he'd end up clogging the channel ole Marvin's digging. Or maybe get stuck inside the earth fill dam." He barely caught January's nod of approval. Surprised him, sort of, that she'd agree with the macabre solution.

As for Ford, he laughed. "Edgar and Billy both?"

"Why not?"

Behind him, January cleared her throat. "That might be a little obvious, don't you think? Unless we could somehow make it appear as though they shot each other."

Shay glanced at her and lifted a brow. "Why would they do that? Weren't they partners?"

She shrugged. "Partners quarrel. Happens all the time."

Ford made a snuffling sound Shay figured was stifled laughter. "She's right, Shay. Them two didn't always get along. Edgar was the wild one, always wanting to shoot somebody or something. Billy took a little less violent route. They were known to argue over it."

"I heard them talking when they showed up here. Billy was going to take my mare and her foal over to Rhodes. Seems Rhodes had put in his catalog order and Billy wanted to play toady." Snorting, Shay nodded down at the body. "This yahoo just wanted to see blood spurt. Guess he got fooled pretty bad. I wouldn't say as they argued about the deal though." He looked up. "That just might work, Miss January, the partners quarreling act, if we set it out right."

Pushing his hat to one side, Ford scratched above his ear and appeared to be thinking. "This is a bad deal, Billings. One way or another,

Sheriff Rhodes will be after your hide when it comes out. And it will come out. Somehow. And when it does, you can bank on the story being twisted."

Shay wondered how Rhodes could twist anything when he, himself, was the only witness. Far as anybody knew, excepting January and now Ford, the pair had never showed up at his place. And he didn't plan on running his mouth with any different story, especially to the sheriff.

"At least there's two fewer bad men to worry about," he said after a moment but Ford gave him a pitying look that made him uneasy.

"Probably won't make much difference," Ford said. "Rhodes, or Hammel, has been hiring. Not loggers, or miners, or engineers, or even ditch diggers like you might expect. He's hiring guns and thinking there'll be a war. That's how I got on." He grinned. "Got a fine letter of recommendation. Paid a feller ten dollars to swear I was as bad a man as he'd ever met."

"Hell," Shay said. "I'd've wrote it for five." It was the closest to levity he could come, considering his boiling anger. Thought he could start a war with the peaceful, hardworking ranchers who lived along this stretch of the river, did he? Kill'em or run'em off and take over from their widows? Not if he could help it. "So, when are you thinking of arresting them two? Or did you plan on waiting until I'm dead?"

Behind him, he heard January suck in a breath. In front of him, Ford's eyes narrowed. "I figure you can take care of yourself for a couple more days. Always have before. I'm looking to build a case against all these yahoos, from the hired guns to Rhodes to, most important, Marvin Hammel. And I ain't got enough on Hammel yet."

"The head of the snake," January said so softly Shay scarcely made out the words.

Bad as he hated to admit it, Ford was right. It would be too easy for Hammel to put the blame on Rhodes. Or the two of them put their heads together and find a way to accuse him of murder. Him or January. God knows they had a grudge against her now, too. He suspected the only reason she was still alive is because they hadn't yet discovered she was the owner of the land at Kindred Creek Crossing and the builder of the new bridge. They still seemed to think he was.

"Sloppy work," he muttered which made Ford say, "Huh?"

"Them still being of the opinion I own the bridge," Shay said. "And since they want it, they keep coming after me."

Ford grew thoughtful. "First time somebody thinks to check at the courthouse, you'll be off the hook."

January jerked, spinning toward her Molly horse and sticking a foot in the stirrup.

Shay held up a hand. "Where you going?"

217

"Home." She settled into her saddle and reined Molly away from the hitch rail. "Before those rowdies find out it's me who is the fly in their ointment and make another attack on the barn and my animals."

"But you . . ." Turns out he was talking to an empty space. Molly, being quicker than he'd thought possible, had spun at January's urging and with a toe to her ribs, shot off down the road at a lope.

While Shay stood there with his mouth hanging open, Ford removed his hat and scratched his head.

"Well," Ford said. "She's some kind of pre-cipitous woman, isn't she? What was that all about? What did she mean about 'the fly in their ointment'?"

"What do you think?" Impatience over Ford's blunder made Shay harsh. "She owns the land on either side of Kindred Creek and she built the damn bridge. They got a grudge against her already. Now they'll be out to make sure she's dead."

Ford scrubbed a hand over his face, taking the curl out of the ends of his mustache. "What I can't figure out is why you wrote that letter to the governor. Why didn't she?"

"Simple. She's a woman," Shay said. "Who'd listen to her? But now she needs protection. It's little enough I can do."

"You're an idiot." Ford shook his head sorrowfully. "So you allow Hammel and Rhodes to believe she's a squatter and you let her stay in the barn out of the goodness of your heart. I suppose Miss January being a handsome woman doesn't figure into it."

Shay's blood started boiling. "I don't have anything to do with what people think. Ain't nobody hardly even know she's here. Hell, Ford, you're as bad a gossip as everyone else in this town. It's no damn wonder she keeps to herself."

"Thought that was the scars."

Shay, clumping toward the barn for the rope off his saddle, shrugged, wincing as the motion pulled at his wound. "The only thing concerns me is that up till now the idea has held Hammel and Rhodes at bay. But somebody is bound to find out and tell them different any time now."

January's abrupt departure left the two men to put their heads together to think of a way out of the dilemma. In a quiet dusk that blanketed the horses in the pasture and set crickets to chirping, the two men decided to follow January's advice.

Or maybe it wasn't advice but only a tongue-in-cheek comment. Nevertheless, they bought into the idea.

"This won't work for long," Ford warned Shay as they, with Ford bearing most of the load, heaved Edgar's body over his saddle and tied him on.

Grimly, Shay spread fresh dirt over the blood stains in his yard, bringing a few buckets of chicken scratchings from the pen to add to the scene. Men looking around wouldn't want to wade through the chicken shit.

Mounting Hoot and leading Edgar's pinto, they rode until, only by keeping a close look-out in the dark, they came to Billy's body.

Ford dismounted. "I can handle him. You stay put. I can see your face glowing white from here. If I didn't know better, I'd say you're the ghost of Eddie Hammel come to haunt us both."

"The hell," Shay said, beyond arguing or thinking Ford any kind of funny. He figured he needed to conserve his energy for when they arranged the bodies as January had suggested.

"Where's a good place to stash them?" Ford asked, breathing a little heavily as he mounted again. The bodies were beginning to stiffen and become hard to handle.

Right, Shay thought. Ford wasn't as familiar with the countryside as he. And he'd been thinking about the problem as they rode, it being pretty hard to think of anything else.

"Where'd you see them last? And when?"

"Noon. In the bunkhouse at Hammel's ranch. They took off a couple hours before I learned what they had in mind. The cook overheard them talking. He commented because they were arguing about something. He don't approve of the way they been acting, by the way, but he keeps his mouth shut and draws his pay."

Shay nodded. "Means they probably rode down this side of the river then without going through town. Wish I knew if anybody saw them."

"What difference does it make?"

"Got an idea on where to dump them. Won't work so good if anybody saw them after they passed that point."

Ford, however, didn't seem as concerned. He shrugged. "Could've been coming or going, right?"

Maybe he was getting too caught up in details, Shay thought, something he didn't have time for. Not when he needed to talk to January again. And he didn't intend for Ford to be part of the conversation.

The four horses clopped through the deepening dusk. Eventually, they came to a place where the rushing river, its tumble loud in the evening silence, fell over huge boulders and ate away at the embankment. They were on Hammel's, formerly Fremont's, land now, a dicey proposition if anyone saw them.

This, Shay thought, looking over the course of the dark river, was the spot Hammel should've put his dam and electricity generators. Here where it ran most swiftly and deeply. Not farther downstream where cows came to drink and ranchers set pumps in the eddies to draw water to their kitchens, gardens, and their stock tanks. If he'd set it here, even the overflow, provided he allowed one, would've kept those ranches with enough water for most purposes. Why hadn't he? Pure cussedness?

"This is it." His quiet voice brought Ford to a halt. "We turn off any minute now."

"What's special about here?"

"We're far enough from Hammel's ranch buildings the sound of gunshots won't reach. There's a deep gully cuts off along here behind these falls. It's hidden from the road and goes behind the hill. Where he could've set up a reservoir without much trouble," he added bitterly. "He doesn't need to flood the whole valley."

"What if Hammel sends out a search party?"

Shay huffed. "The way them boys wandered around shooting my place up and harassing Miss January while looking for me? I don't think so. Not right away, anyhow. I think that's what they were hired to do. I'll wager he expected Billy to disappear after killing me."

Ford's nod showed only because it was silhouetted against the dark sky. "You could be right. Welp, lead the way. Let's get this pair off-loaded."

Wouldn't you know, Shay thought, it was at this very moment they heard hoofbeats on the road ahead of them. Coming their way and coming fast.

"Hellfire," Ford said softly, his head cocked. "You hear that?"

Shay pressed the reins against Hoot's neck. "Follow me. Quick now. Get those ponies moving."

The turn-off to the area he wanted was just ahead. Too bad it meant they were riding toward whomever was on the road with them. The outlaw's horses with their stiff burdens proved reluctant carriers and slow along with it. Even so, presently, he led Ford through a narrow, innocuous-looking opening to the gully and when they'd ridden around a bend, held up his hand to stop all telltale movement. No more than a minute later the riders passed behind them. One of the riders was whooping and hollering.

"Drunk." Ford spoke softly.

Shay's jaw was set, his voice grim. "One is."

"Probably Carter," Ford said. "He hides a flask and nips from it pretty steady. The rest act like they don't notice."

Shay worried one of the other men, one maybe not so drunk, would smell the fresh dust of his and Ford's passage and think to investigate. He guessed there were six or seven riders if the sound of the horses was anything to go by. All of them trigger-happy fools most likely.

But minutes ticked by, the noise fading into the night along with his tension.

"All right. Let's get these yahoos arranged."

He nudged Hoot and they started off again.

The gully opened out into a little meadow, one which, if Hammel had chosen to site his dam properly, would've been flooded by now. A rising moon illuminated a thirty-acre spot area where the grass grew high. It was studded with arrowroot balsam, the color of the yellow flowers true under the starlight. Boulders studded the area.

Shay pointed to one of the boulders. "Looks like a good spot for him." He indicated Edgar and Ford obligingly dismounted and cut the rope holding the outlaw over his saddle. The body dropped with a thud, landing face up behind the boulder. Shay nodded approval as the pinto shied.

"I like the middle of the meadow for this one." Ford led the bay into the tallest grass and again cut ropes. Billy landed on his face, his arms flung down with the palms up, the bullet hole in his back clearly showing. Ford placed the dead outlaw's revolver near his hand. "Bullets from this'll match yours. If anybody even looks at the wound in Edgar's throat. And you pull out his rifle and drop it down close to him. That ought to do. Then let's get out of here before we leave tracks a little girl could follow."

He didn't need to urge Shay twice. In a matter of minutes, they were headed back the way they'd come, leaving the outlaws' horses loose to find their way home.

"Where do you suppose those yahoos were headed?" Shay's question came out of the dark. Made uneasy now he'd had time to think about their near miss with Hammel's rowdies, worry flooded into his mind.

Ford, riding beside him, gave a start as if he'd just woken from a nap. "Dunno, now you mention it." He was silent, head cocked as if listening for more than the crash and fall of the river running beside them. Then, after a moment where the horse's strides lengthened out, he said, "But I know where I'd be going."

"Yeah? Where?" But Shay's voice indicated he knew and without thinking twice of his own weakness and tiredness, his heels touched Hoot's ribs, asking for more speed.

Even so, Ford answered. "Guess I'd be paying Miss January a visit."

Their horses broke into a lope.

CHAPTER 17

What, January wondered as she lay awake listening to the sounds of the night, did Shay and Ford plan to do with those bodies? How would Shay explain them, and the blood and the whole mixed up mess, if anyone came looking? Anyone meaning Marvin Hammel and Sheriff Elroy Rhodes, of course. Sheriff Rhodes wouldn't dare . . . would he? Or was he so sure of Hammel and his importance to the muckety-muck mining interests that he could do whatever he wanted, secure in knowing no repercussions awaited. Murder, outright theft, coercion, threats, assault . . . the list went on and on. Whatever it took to get ahead.

Who was there to stop them after all? Ford Tervo, the governor's special envoy, providing he was even trustworthy? Shay Billings, a small rancher? January Schutt, a nonentity if there ever was one?

Turning restlessly on the cot where Shay had recently spent so many days, January flung her hand over her eyes and tried to sleep. Lord knows she was tired enough. She reached down beside the bed, touching her dog's warm fur. Lucky Pen, snoring the night away on the rug by January's narrow cot.

What were they up to, Shay and Ford? Should she have stayed and helped? Was Shay strong enough to exert himself the way he was no doubt doing?

The vision of him lying on the ground, his eyes closed, face pale, returned to her. That and the way her heart had frozen for a moment, thinking him dead.

Just the thought of my hard work in saving him going to waste, that's all.

Somewhere in the distance, thunder rumbled and January squeezed her eyes more tightly closed.

Until it struck her.

The noise couldn't be thunder. The skies were clear tonight, the stars shining and the moon out in force. So the rumble must be horses on the road. Several horses, still on the other side of the river but nearing her bridge. Ridden with a no-good purpose. She sensed menace with every fiber of her being.

Shivering, she sprang from the cot, slid into her trousers, stuck her feet in boots and buckled on a belt heavy with a holstered .38. Cartridges studded the belt. A large knife swung on the other side for balance. In all, a contraption both unhandy and uncomfortable. Pen rose to stand beside her, fur ruffled, a rumble of her own gathering in her throat. Pen always recognized a threat. January could trust the aging dog for that.

The barn, even in the process of falling in on itself, was still too large for her to defend if too many came after her all at once. And if a couple determined souls did succeed in gaining the interior and managed to avoid her clever booby traps, she'd likely be the one ensnared by her own deterrent.

"What shall we do, eh, Pen?" Her whisper caused the dog to prick her ears and look at her. "No, I don't know either. I think I've about had enough. I'm ready to run."

She spoke those cowardly words even as she darted from one barn window to another. Days ago, she'd taken—stolen, really—a rifle from the man she clubbed on the head during the previous attack. She'd stowed the rifle just inside the barn's front door, ready to grab if anyone got too close. A shotgun leaned against the wall near the secret escape hatch. She checked the other shotgun, the one that'd almost nailed a man the night three of them broke in. It was set and ready to go.

Were her preparations enough? A chill made her fingers stiff. Her chin wobbled until she set her jaw.

So, grinding her teeth together, she forced her fingers to flex.

Hooves drummed on the bridge, a hollow sound that echoed in her chest. It signaled the riders' arrival on her side of Kindred Creek. Oddly enough, they halted down there. All of them. A mutter of voices, low enough she'd never have heard them if she'd been sleeping, reached her ears.

"Come, Pen," she said. "Get away from the door. Stay with me."

As though she knew what her mistress meant, Pen pressed against January's legs.

"Good girl."

The night, when January stuck her head outside the ramshackle barn door, provided enough light for her to see the group of horses and riders stopped at the post where the toll receptacle was anchored. They milled around but she didn't think they were paying the fare. No indeed.

In fact, she heard the screech of nails as someone yanked the can away and threw it on the ground. Some of them laughed and a louder voice told them to shut up.

A second later, the flare of a match made a tiny pinprick of light. A few moments later, a flame leapt into the air as a man held the match to a torch that must've been treated with pitch or tar. There'd been a torch on the ground at Shay's cabin, too. The order of the day, she supposed. "Burn them out."

Flames swam and blurred as the first torch passed from the first man, then a second, and a third, until torches lit the night as bright as day.

She could see them clearly now. One figure

she recognized as the sheriff. The others were unknown to her. A fast count indicated seven individuals. Seven!

"Son of a . . ." How am I supposed to fight so many?

Pen looked up at her.

"I think we'd better run." January lay her hand on Pen's head. The hand trembled violently, her whole arm shaking. "That'd be the smart thing."

Smart, yes. But it wasn't what she wanted to do. She'd created a safe haven—or at least she'd thought it safe—in which to live. She'd made it her own when there was nowhere else to go. She had a garden, animals, rocks collected with which to build a real house. She had a bridge that she'd built with her own two hands, one meant to bring acceptance of her from those who used it.

She'd saved a man's life and his home.

Anger coursed through her.

This was hers and she didn't intend to give it up. Not without a fight.

January wasn't even aware she'd picked up the nearby rifle as she looked outside. Nor that she'd jacked a cartridge into the rifle's firing chamber. Without letting herself think twice, she raised the rifle to her shoulder and took aim a couple feet below one of the men's firebrands.

"Should be about right."

Her breath held, then released half. Her finger squeezed slowly, gently.

The report broke against her eardrums and even Pen, already half-deaf, flinched.

A man screamed as the torch fell away to flare at his horse's front feet. He clutched at his arm as the horse jumped away from the fire. The others milled about. Shouts arose. No one seemed to grasp one of their group had been shot—at first.

January saw that much but by then she was already retreating to one of the empty barn windows where she fired off another shot before moving on again. Pen stuck with her as though glued to her thigh.

A flurry of shots thudded into the side of the barn where she'd been only seconds before. January almost laughed. It'd taken long enough for them to figure it out but now it was Retaliation with a capital R. The attackers emptied their guns, shooting through the open doorway to spend their ammunition against the thick wood of a badly-chewed manger.

"Six," she said to Pen. "One down, six to go."

Still impossible odds.

The six charged the barn, horses at a dead run.

"Down, Pen," January commanded, following her own order and dropping to her belly at the right of the open doorway. A barrel, used at one time to store feed away from the mice, sat there, the metal bands loose. As shelter, it wasn't much. She poked the rifle barrel around it and as the first rider showed himself, she fired upward at a thick body.

Her bullet missed him, only to strike another who rode on his far side and slightly behind. This one yelped and dropped his torch where it briefly glowed on the ground before fading out. The rider remained in the saddle but rode off toward the first casualty who remained down by the bridge, sitting at the edge of the road and sobbing.

The sheriff's voice rose above the others, all of whom seemed to be shouting. January heard a rebel yell, a warrior's ululating cry, a great deal of cursing, and exhortations to "Kill him. Kill them both. Burn'em out." The last came from Rhodes.

So they didn't know Shay had left. Good for him; maybe not so good for her.

In a group, they swept around the side of the barn, black silhouettes against the night. She got up and ran, her intention to cross the open space prior to them coming around again but before she and Pen could take up a defensive position, one of the torches sailed through a small side window, shattering glass and spreading fire. The torch fell into the dust but it was close to the barn wall and before she could get there to stomp the blaze out, the dried out wood caught with a flash.

Pen barked, high and loud.

"Shh, Pen. I see it." January knew someone

was bound to enter the barn and attempt to chase her into the light. Soon, before it got too hot. Oh, he wouldn't penetrate far. Only far enough to prevent her from breaking free. Five men remained. If he was any kind of leader at all, Rhodes would order them to surround the place, to guard the windows so she couldn't get out. They wouldn't know about the escape hatch although the sheriff might suspect.

"Dammit." Smoke already caught at the back of her throat, scraping out a cough. "Dammit all to hell."

If she and Pen were to survive, they had to leave now, before the sheriff and his men were set. Give the fire enough time and they'd be able to pick her off at their leisure.

"C'mon." Touching Pen's head, she headed for her room and the hidden back entry. It was as she passed the booby trap she'd depended on to save her that she spotted the gleam of the almost-finished table she'd been building. All that work, the fine wood, the love and care she'd lavished on it. All wasted. Resentful tears flushed smoke from her eyes.

Apparently this old place would never be done with her. Not until she was dead.

The crackle of the growing flames, the whoosh of downdraft-fueled outbreaks warned her there wasn't much time. She'd have to leave everything except the small satchel that contained her small store of money and the deeds and certificates proving her claim to the land.

Those took a mere second to grab, another couple seconds to the exit, and then she and Pen were scooting through the narrow opening behind the fallen roof that sheltered the exit.

Heat seared her back as she took one last look outside.

Pen whined.

"Yes. I know." January saw nothing. The burning barn lit the night as bright as day. Thankfully, it wasn't far to the first bit of cover. As long as she and the dog got that far, they'd be able to work their way to the riverbank and make good their escape. "Get ready. We'll have to run," she said and stepped outside.

It took only a moment to know she'd made a mistake although, really, there'd been no choice. Burn or—

The bullet caught her along the calf of her right leg, cutting a furrow and taking her down as though chopped off at the knees. Pain set every nerve in her body ablaze, no real fire needed. The satchel dropped to the ground and tumbled into the dark.

But that wasn't the worst. No. The worst was Pen—good, loyal Pen—gathering herself to leap for the man who stepped out of the darkness.

Sheriff Elroy Rhodes, who lifted his revolver and took aim at the air-bound dog.

CHAPTER 18

A prolonged rattle of gunfire reached Shay's ears a few minutes before the bridge came into sight. Reining Hoot down from a lope, he cocked his head, listening.

"Hear that?" he asked Ford, riding slightly behind him.

Ford answered grimly. "I ain't deaf. Sure I do. What do you think . . . ?"

Shay set Hoot in motion again, urging the horse back into a lope, never mind that both men's horses were lathered and drawing deep breaths. Breathing nearly as hard as his horse, he leaned over the saddle, unconsciously favoring his hurt side.

Spurring his horse even with Hoot, Ford didn't finish the question.

Shay answered anyway; the intent, if not the specifics. "I don't think. I know. Just like we figured, that sheep-eating rat Elroy Rhodes has gone after January, guns drawn. He probably believes I'm still at the barn."

Ford swore as he drew his rifle from the saddle scabbard. "You suppose she's shooting back?"

Shay grinned, a simple baring of his teeth as much grimace as humor. "You bet your britches. Doubt we'd be hearing gunfire if she wasn't."

Once around a final bend in the road, they slowed as they approached the bridge, its raw new lumber pale against the darkness of road and sky. Beyond that, the glimmer of flames rising from the north side of the barn lit a broad area around it. Light glaring through the wide open door revealed a couple men caught inside trying to escape the growing conflagration. One made two dashes forward only to have flames drive him back both times.

Shay swore. "Stupid bastards set the barn on fire and got their own men trapped."

His attention fixed ahead, he wasn't even aware of the wounded man writhing in the road like a snake cut in two by a wagon wheel. Or not until Hoot took a little leap and jumped over the body, his bounce claiming Shay's attention at last.

The man hollered, clipped possibly by one of Hoot's hooves, earning himself no more than a dismissive glance from Ford who also passed him by. Then they were pounding up to the barn and drawing to a halt just beyond the fire's light. None of the men there paid them any attention. They were hollering advice to the men inside, some of it contradictory.

"Goddamn," Ford shouted. "What if she can't get out?"

Shay refused to believe it. Those shots he'd heard. They hadn't come from inside.

"Not her. There's another way to escape, back

of the barn," he said, maybe before time because just then the guns went silent.

For all of ten seconds.

Then came a single shot from behind the barn and his heart seemed to stop.

Flames leapt for the edge of the roof. Shay thought the wood must've been doused with oil considering the fire's quick spread as it bit into the shingles. One of the men Shay'd thought trapped inside threw his arm over his eyes and surged forward. Staggering through the doors, he dropped to his knees, coughing as though to expel his lungs from his body. The other man followed the first's example. Shirt on fire, he ran from the barn screaming. Beating at his smoldering trousers with his hat once outside, he succeeded in fanning the flames to virulent life.

Quick as a man can think, Shay freed his rope from the saddle tie and tossed the loop around the man, dragging him down into the dirt and putting out the fire. He doubted he'd ever hear any thanks.

Loose horses pelted about, frightened by the noise and the snap and pop of flames. One horse bore a rider who, taking a look at Shay's set face, dug in his spurs and raced away down the road toward town. A couple riderless animals following herd instinct dashed after him.

Parked on the side of the barn opposite the fire, January's lowboy provided cover for two men who finally recognized Shay and Ford as an opposing force. One hurried to reload his pistol, the other took shaky aim at Ford.

Shay dropped the end of his lariat and pulled his .44. He fired off a shot that put a bullet in the shooter's mid-section and sent him toppling to the ground bellowing with pain.

"Quick," he said to Ford. "Around back. If she—"

But he wouldn't think about ifs.

Hoot rounded the corner first, Shay poised to fire as he reined in the horse. Ford drew up alongside.

"What the hell?" Ford's eyes narrowed against the smoke.

No one was there. No Rhodes, no January, no dog.

Only the fire crackling behind them as it consumed the barn at Kindred Creek Crossing.

Rhodes's shot knocked January sprawling. Pure dumb luck resulted in her right hand closing on a fist-sized rock. It could even have been the pain in her leg that made her fingers clench around the rock and, in shocked reflex, heave it at Rhodes.

He may have seen the rock coming and tried to dodge. January would never know but for whatever reason, it took too long for him to fire at Pen as she sprang toward him. January's aim was good. The rock spun through the air, knocking the gun from his hand at the precise moment his finger squeezed the trigger. The bullet went wild, whirling into the night and missing both woman and dog.

Or maybe Rhodes was just a lousy shot.

"Bitch," he hissed at her. Then Pen was on him, teeth bared, her growl ferocious enough to—judging by the way he yelled—strike fear in the sheriff.

"Pen!" January seized her chance, regaining her feet the moment the stone left her hand. "Leave it. Let's go."

Pen, busy savaging the sheriff's arm, got in a few good nips before obeying January's frantic command.

Woman and dog ran, Rhodes's curses as he searched for the gun following them into the night.

They headed for the river, cutting behind the shed where January had buffaloed one of the outlaw gang a few days earlier. Cut off from the light of the burning barn, the path leading to the irrigation pumphouse seemed darker, the ground underfoot more slippery than usual. Her breath came raggedly. She stumbled often, limping and listing to one side. The inside of her boot squished with blood gathering there.

She kept going. There was another trap at the pumphouse. One meant to keep animals from disturbing the flow of water rather than to discourage humans but she'd have no objection to Rhodes falling into it. The trap involved a spring, a clamp, and a twisty lock. If caught, he'd find himself pinned until someone arrived to free him.

If caught.

He wasn't giving up on her being the one caught. January, hearing him floundering along the path at her rear, turned to see him maybe fifty feet behind. Too close. Then his boots slid on the stony riverbank and she saw him go down. He shouted out his rage.

Good. She hoped he broke a leg but even slowing him down helped her surge ahead, sheer willpower keeping her leg from collapsing beneath her.

Her heart pumped frantically, sounding in her ears like the beat of a parade drum.

This frenzied chase was an eerie reminder of a night thirteen years ago. This panic-stricken run toward the river, seeking the shelter of one of her hideouts? She'd tried the same thing then only to have her plan fail. Years ago, the man after her had been her own grandfather. The man had gone mad as the proverbial hatter and had seen in the ten-year-old child the embodiment of his dead wife whom he'd hated. To this day, January didn't know why. Her dad hadn't known why. Maybe Grandfather Shutt hadn't known why.

Once he'd cornered her, he described the

deranged thoughts swirling in his mind. Terrified, she hadn't really comprehended his mutterings when she was ten. Oh, she'd understood well enough that he intended to murder her. Now she understood that years before he'd murdered her grandmother, too. He'd wanted to use January, a little girl, as a woman. He'd wanted to break her into pieces. But first he wanted to mark her, to prove she belonged to him and he could do whatever he willed.

So she'd run down this same path, toward this same goal, seeking safety. Trying to hide. Trying to live.

At last, the pumphouse's small stone structure loomed out of the dark. They'd arrived.

Her granddad had caught her, of course, right here on this same spot. He'd done the marking first, savoring her pain, her terror, her begging. Most of all, her sobs that mingled tears with blood. He'd even liked hearing her scream, encouraging her to "pluck up the volume." She thought she'd die. Maybe even wanted to. And then, out of nowhere, her dad appeared, home from town hours early because he'd known his own father couldn't be trusted for long around his little girl.

Her dad had shot his own father dead and buried him and all his wickedness in the woods at the edge of the pasture. And then her dad set the house on fire, gathered January, fainting by then and barely conscious, into his arms and ridden with her to Dr. LeBret. The doctor stitched up her wounds but, like Granddad had planned, she was forever marked, the scar tracing out the letter S not only on her cheek but on her heart.

Dad had come too late, when all they could do was run from the consequences. And though he'd tried to escape his own guilt in leaving her, he never quite succeeded. He spent the rest of his life trying to make up for the mistake.

There wasn't anybody going to show up and save her this time. There was only herself and Pen against Sheriff Rhodes, his anger and his gun.

The dog's body spread warmth under her hand. January realized the old dog was taking her weight, holding her up. And that just wouldn't do.

"Good girl." She mouthed the words soundlessly, standing free of the dog.

Best case, in her opinion, was if Sheriff Rhodes were to fall in the creek and drown. Unlikely. Kindred Creek wasn't exactly a raging river. The only time the banks ran full was in the spring when the snow went off in the mountains. Summer brought low water, no doubt why Hammel and Rhodes were trying to seal off every bit they could buy or steal and store it in the reservoir for their power plant. Preferably steal, going by recent events.

Still, the water in the eddy feeding her pump-house and irrigation system was deeper than most places. A quick push might be all he needed to discourage his murderous inclination. She'd be glad to give that push, the only thing she could think to do, and she'd bet Pen would help.

Silently, she and Pen stepped back into the shadows. Sinking down, she sat with her back against a boulder and waited for Rhodes to appear.

"Where'd they go?" Ford shifted in his saddle, trying to look all ways at once. The burning barn separated them from Rhodes's men.

"Listen." Shay cocked his head toward the river, trying to make sense of sounds that seemed out of place. "Hear that?"

"All I hear is a bunch of second-rate outlaws back yonder crying their eyes out, every one ripe for arrest. Which I will be glad to do."

"Not until January is safe."

"Agreed." A second later, Ford said, "Hear what?"

Shay thought he'd caught a sound of a commotion just beyond the edge of the pasture where the ground broke over to the riverbank. A bellow, he thought, and a clatter as though someone had fallen. It had been a surprised man's sort of bellow.

"This way," he said. Beaten-down grass

243

showed the path January had worn with her many trips to the river. On horseback, they needed only a minute to reach a steep drop-off down to the water. Shay dismounted, exhaustion causing him to lean against Hoot and wish he could stay there the night. Damn, but he was weak, his reserves used up.

Ford appeared beside him, following his lead by dismounting. "You all right?" he asked.

"Sure," Shay lied, straightening. "We'll leave the horses here and go on foot now."

"Yeah, but go where? Which way?"

Be damned if I know. Shay didn't want to say so but Ford's guess was as good as his. He hadn't ever walked January's property. All he knew was what she'd mentioned in passing while he'd been laid up in her barn. Given her secretive nature, that wasn't much. Wasn't enough.

"Do you see anything? Or anybody?" Shay looked out over swift-moving dark water as it splashed over rocks, surprisingly noisy when he wanted to listen. But he heard only the creek and he saw nobody.

Ford shrugged and shook his head "no."

Shay scowled. "All right. You go left, I'll go right."

Nodding, Ford eyed him. "You be careful. You ain't in tip-top shape, you know."

Shay did know. And that he'd be better off saving his breath for something better than saying so. He scrambled down the bank to the creek's edge where, to his surprise, he found another of those faint paths. At one time, for instance when the Schutt place had been in daily use, he imagined the paths well-worn. On this one, even the dim light provided evidence of recent use; trampled grass, turned over rocks. He followed the signs, hoping it led somewhere other than a flat spot where animals came to drink.

And then he knew it did as dark smudges showed on the grass. Shay bent and stuck his finger on one of them before wiping the finger on his britches.

Blood. He'd known it would be.

But whose blood? January's or Rhodes's?

CHAPTER 19

January despaired, knowing she'd left signs any halfway competent tracker could follow as she made her escape. Pen, her fellow escapee, sat at her side watching with worried eyes as January wrapped a handkerchief around her wounded leg and tightened the ends. Her eyes closed, allowing the ebb and roll of the rushing stream to wash over her, bringing with it a strange, threatening lassitude. Lord, but she was so tired.

"It'll be all right," January whispered to the dog. "Don't you worry. We'll get out of this. Anyway, what's another scar in my collec—" She broke off, her eyes popping open as footsteps approached.

"Hello, what have we here?" The man laughed, low and menacing as though he'd discovered some destructive secret about her and couldn't wait to tell. "Could this be blood I see on this rock?"

Damn Rhodes! How had he managed to find her so fast? She'd hoped for a few minutes to gather herself and renew her courage. Instead, like a fool, she'd led him right to her. Pray her trap worked.

Her fingers clenched in Pen's fur. It took all her strength to keep the dog still when Pen tried to regain her feet. "Shh," she said, using the boulder behind her for support as she rose into a crouch. With every heartbeat her leg burned as if jabbed by a red-hot poker, but it held.

"I know you're here," he called, as puffed-up and arrogant as though she hadn't bested him and gotten away only minutes ago. "It won't do you any good to hide. I'll find you soon enough." He sniggered. "Or maybe I'll just find your dead body. I seen you're losing blood. A dribble with every step you take. Looks like you might could bleed to death if I wait long enough. A pity."

January remained silent. He was trying to scare her but it wouldn't work.

After a pause, he said, "You might've landed one lucky blow but don't count on it happening again. If you give yourself up, the only one dead tonight will be that damn dog. Oh, yeah. And Shay Billings. My men have already taken care of him. Barn's on fire and he ain't getting out. It's just you, missy, so which is it gonna be? You or the dog?" The snigger came again. "Last chance."

January welcomed the anger flooding into her system. It lent a fresh surge of energy, reminding her that as cocksure as Rhodes might be, he didn't know everything. For instance, he didn't know Shay not only wasn't in the barn but he wasn't there at all. And he didn't know that as soon as she'd stopped running and had a chance to tighten the handkerchief around her leg, the bleeding had almost ceased. She might feel a little faint but she wasn't running dry. Not yet.

However—and here was the part she didn't like—in order to catch Rhodes in her trap, she had to coax him into its vicinity. And the lynchpin of all such plans: the trap required baiting. Which left two choices. Herself or Pen.

She may have made a sound because Rhodes went still, his head tilted into a listening position. Pen trembled beneath January's hand.

The bait isn't going to be Pen. He'd shoot her at first sight and not think twice.

January reached her hand to where Pen could see her making the stay signal. Slowly, muscles tense and her reluctance clear, the dog lowered herself to the down position.

The holster with January's .38 bumped against her thigh, making her wince anew. She hesitated to draw the weapon. She didn't want to shoot Rhodes. Well, truthfully, she did but she had mixed feelings about him being dead. She wouldn't weep over his body, that much was certain. But she had the thought he might come in handier alive if he could be persuaded to talk about Hammel, the Langley boy's murder, and his part in this water-stealing conspiracy.

It was a mighty big "if."

When the sheriff next spoke, he'd moved a few

yards closer. Pen wriggled at the sound of his voice although she remained in place.

"There's a limit to my patience," he said.

Yes. January could tell.

His voice grew harsher. "I ain't got time for these parlor tricks of yours. How you got out of the barn is a good one, even if you couldn't haul Billings along with you. Bet you're crying your eyes out about that, aren't you? That what's holding you up? See, you ain't the only one doing some crying. Soon as those Inman sisters hear about Billings burning to death, they'll be bawling all over themselves, too. Bet you didn't know about them, did you?"

What was he trying to do, stir the jealousy pot? Striving to rouse her to action? It wouldn't work. She'd met the Inman sisters which meant his ruse had no meaning. Quiet as an eight-legged ant, January peeped over the top of the boulder.

Rhodes stood outlined against a background of river and sky. From the angle of his head, he seemed to be looking right at her.

Ducking back, she drew in a breath. *Did he see me? I'm not ready.*

Her courage was waning, seeping away like water through sand. If she didn't put her plan in motion now, she never would. She'd cower here until he came for her and then she would be obliged to shoot him. She touched the pistol on her hip, certain that shooting a sheriff was not a wise move no matter how much he deserved it.

Rhodes stood on a round-topped boulder, one that lent him height. He kept twisting one way and then another as if trying to catch her out. Perhaps he thought he'd flush her into the open if he waited long enough and appeared threatening enough.

He did appear plenty threatening but the longer she watched, the more convinced she became he had no idea she crouched almost within touching distance. So. Bait. She needed him to come closer to where the stream took a sharp curve that left a deep backwater at the inlet to the pumphouse's natural enclosure. Waves lashed there now, gurgling as the barricade held the stream to its channel.

Giving Pen a reinforcing signal to stay, January tensed, ready for the moment when Rhodes turned the other way. When he did, she slipped from her shelter, stopping behind a cottonwood tree whose branches overhung the pumphouse. Ducking down, she waited for shots that didn't come.

"Missy," he called again, stomping from one boulder to the next. And, as luck would have it, in the right direction. "I'm tired of this game. Come out."

He lined up just about perfectly as long as he came straight at her. Her job as bait was to make sure he did. Then, at just the right moment, she'd jump to the pumphouse roof and trigger the handle that opened the inlet. It was how she irrigated her garden. Water would pour in and, if everything happened correctly, Rhodes'd be caught by the deep water and the foot snare. Placed to keep animals and fish out of the pump, she had no doubt the trap would work as well on a man as it did on beaver. The water wasn't deep enough to drown him as long as he was even a little wise but the snare would keep him from getting out and taking up the fight.

January waited until his attention wandered again before she jumped to the stony pumphouse roof. Pain radiated through her leg and, for a moment, her vision turned black.

Hearing her feet land and gravel shift, he spun to face her, surprise large on his face. "There you are." He grinned.

Bait, January reminded herself, doing her best not to flinch. Not even as the grin disappeared and he said, "Gotta say I was getting impatient. Time to wind this up."

The way his eyes kept shifting back and forth puzzled her until he said, "Where's that damn dog?"

He's afraid of Pen. The knowledge came as a satisfying surprise.

"He comes at me, I'll shoot him dead," Rhodes said. "Fact is, I'm gonna shoot'em dead anyways."

He seemed to take pleasure in announcing his intention.

"It's a she," January said.

"What?"

"I said it's a she. The dog is female."

Rhodes took an angry step forward. "Who the hell cares? I'm just telling you . . .'"

"I care." January's voice rose over his. "If you want me to give up, the least you can do is get my dog's gender right."

"Oh, fer my Aunt Hattie's sake." He raised his gun, pointing it at her. "You're not as clever as you think you are, by Gawd. Get over here."

Bait. January spread her arms wide so he could see she held no weapon. "Why should I make it easy? You want me, come and get me."

It was an invitation Elroy Rhodes had to accept. He fixed her with a hard glare and jumped between rocks until he stood only a couple steps away.

January refused to flinch, remaining in place as though rooted to the spot. Not . . . quite . . . yet. Her vision went from bright to dark even as movement seemed to flicker out on the path. Another of his men? She had to get this done.

"Turn around," he said.

"Why?" Her voice quavered, not all, she was ashamed to say, an act. Her legs felt weak when they had to be strong. "So you can shoot me in the back? What's the matter? Are you afraid of looking me in the eyes?"

That's all it took. With a growl like an animal, he jumped across the final gap and onto the stone ledge guarding the pump enclosure. Sure of himself, Rhodes grabbed for her. As if it were an afterthought, she slapped away his hand and at the same time stomped on the handle hidden in the gravel.

With an abrupt thud, the trap released. Two things happened. First, Rhodes's pistol went off and second, the ledge let go beneath his weight. It took him down. Creek water surged in an overwhelming gush over his head, submerging him in the deepest part of the pool.

He shouted out a curse muffled by the water, his panic telling her the snare had caught his foot. Bobbing to the surface, his arms flailed. He'd dropped his gun and his squinty eyes were wide with shock.

"Help!" he yelled, his voice tinny with fear. "Help me. You little whore, get me out of here." He went under, then bobbed to the surface, gasping. "I'm gonna kill you!"

A low chuckle came from the path beyond the inlet.

January spun, reaching for her pistol. The dark figure of a man made his way toward them over the rocky riverbank, moving a little slow. It didn't matter. January recognized him even by starlight.

Shay.

She went weak with relief.

"Not much incentive in that, Elroy," he said. Then to January, "You are one smart, inventive woman, January Schutt. You protect yourself better with your traps and tricks than most men can do with a gun."

He studied Rhodes's panicked floundering in the pool. Every once in a while, the sheriff's head would sink under the water and he'd come up slapping the surface and spitting. And using up his breath shouting invective which January did her best to ignore.

Shay gestured at Rhodes. "He gonna drown?"

January couldn't seem to raise the energy to care. Dispassionately, she eyed the sheriff before shrugging. "Only if he's too stupid to hang onto the edge."

The sheriff went under again, cutting off his latest curses in mid-breath.

"Looks like he might be." Shay shook his head.

January was tired beyond measure. It took real effort to look alert when a rattle of stones indicated someone approaching on the run. "Who . . . ?" she managed to say before the words died on her lips.

Shay faced the newcomer, huffing out an amused greeting. "About time you got here," he said as Ford pounded up to them. "What took you so long? You missed the fun."

Ford stopped to study the sheriff's predicament as Rhodes floundered in the pool. "I heard a shot. Who's shooting who?"

They'd gotten back to the barn a half-hour after fishing Rhodes out of the channel in front of the pumphouse. The endeavor hadn't gone smoothly with the sheriff fighting every step of the way and complaining of his inefficient "deputies."

January considered he should've said gang, a more accurate term by far in her opinion.

Ford, having improvised a complicated wrist cuff out of rope to encourage Rhodes to order, interrogated the sheriff as they watched the destroyed structure die down to embers and ash. January listened, too tired to speak.

After a while, even Ford became disgruntled at the sheriff's stubborn silence.

"He's a tough nut to crack," he said, coming over to where Shay and January sat.

"Should've left him in the water." Shay grinned. "He didn't much like getting wet."

"Yeah, so maybe I'll throw him back in." Ford didn't, wrestling Rhodes onto his bay's saddle and the two of them taking the road into town instead.

January perched on the end of the lowboy much like Shay had done this morning. The wagon was miraculously unharmed except for a few scorch marks in the wood. The sparks had flown freely for a while. One of her legs, bent at the knee, helped balance the wounded leg she kept propped on the low side-rail. She relied on the premise the height would keep the blood from pooling in her foot and the pain at bay. Not that she found the treatment particularly effective.

But even Dr. LeBret had advocated something like that when he'd discussed Shay's treatment with her. It's why she'd put a folded blanket under Shay's feet as he lay on the cot.

Actually, she didn't think her wound was all that bad as long as it didn't go septic; it was just bloody. And she had to admit it hurt like Hades.

The barn was truly gone now, with no chance of resurrection. What thirteen years of winter snow and summer sun couldn't do, January thought sadly, Rhodes and his men had done in less than an hour with a few firebrands. The fire destroyed every one of her personal possessions along with it—except for the lowboy and maybe a few other pieces of equipment stored out of doors. Not that any of them would do much good with Ernie's harness and Molly's saddle incinerated. At least her animals survived. Ernie, Molly, the cow, some chickens, and most favored of all, Pen, who lay sleeping next to her and panting gently.

January's hand drifted up and scratched behind the dog's ears.

And her bridge. The apparent cause of all this. That survived, too. Down on the road, the two men she'd wounded made dark lumps on the wood. One of them didn't move at all; the other twitched every once in a while.

Ford had promised to bring Dr. LeBret back with him. And, at best, round up a few men they could trust to do something about Rhodes and these others that didn't include lynching them. Ford, being a Deputy U.S. Marshal, didn't want to be part of anything smacking of vigilante justice. He planned to incarcerate Rhodes in one of his own jail cells when no one was looking.

January gave a great, shuddering sigh, one that carried to Shay who sat with his back against the lowboy's right wheel. He was keeping an eye on a couple of outlaws who sat slumped in the trampled dirt right next to a badly-burned dead man. The dying fire glowed behind them.

"You all right, January?" Shay turned to look at her. His face was pale and he slumped as if exhausted.

A question she should be asking him.

Every corpuscle in January's body shouted "no" but she said, "Yes. Don't worry about me. It's just . . ." Just the question spinning round and round in her brain, that's all. The one that kept screaming, "What am I going to do now? Live under my bridge like a troll?"

"You should try to sleep," he said, advice more easily handed out than followed.

Unexpected—more, unwanted—tears spurted. Quickly, before Shay could see, she lowered her head onto her drawn-up knee.

January's heavy sigh signified despair no matter what she said. Shay heard it as plain as if it'd been recorded on an Edison gramophone.

"Don't worry," he said. "We've got them on the run. Quick as Tervo rounds up Hammel, we can all get back to normal." His assurance rang false even to himself. He suspected Hammel might be politically as well as monetarily powerful enough to overcome even murder, arson, and theft. Shay wouldn't be surprised but what he'd blame Rhodes for the whole shebang and make it stick.

As for January, where would she live now that her barn had burned to the ground and most of her resources destroyed?

The outlaw nearest Shay racked out a cough and spat into the dirt. "That's what you think, buster. Hammel has too much invested to let a few stump-ranch cowboys like you and Bent Langley and that traitor Turk stop him."

Evidently, Ford had told the gang to call him Turk. Little did they know it was his ethnicity not his name.

Shay didn't bother to look at the man. "Shut up."

The outlaw ignored Shay. "He has a bounty on you, ya know."

This did draw Shay's attention. "Bounty?"

"Yep. He's gonna own this bridge and this river one way or another. With you dead, he'll just come in and take it over. You want to live, you should get the hell out of this country."

"Only ones leaving are you and this bunch of lowlife rowdies. You're going straight to prison." He'd had trouble recognizing Jonas Bennett, Hammel's foreman—now turned outlaw—through all the soot and dirt covering his face. Shay'd never cared for the man. He was hard on horses and cows.

January lifted her gaze to Bennett's ugly face. "Who takes over if Hammel is dead?"

Bennett spat again and shrugged.

January sighed. "Then I hope he dies."

"Don't count your chickens," Bennett said. "Rhodes mighta been his right hand man but the boss can take care of himself. What I'm saying is, he ain't crippled. Not by a long shot. As for you, Billings, you ain't gonna be around long enough to bother him any. Me and the others, including Rhodes, will be back in the saddle before you can whistle Ma Blushing Rosie. Count on it."

"Enough." Shay got to his feet and paced. He was restless beyond his tiredness with an overwhelming feeling he needed to get home. When Bennett said his boss could take care of himself, what had he meant? Were there more of Hammel's hired gunmen preparing to wipe him out?

January broke the silence at the end of his third circuit. "Why haven't you told them about the bridge, Shay?"

Shay shook his head, making a shushing sound at her. He hoped she'd take the hint and remain silent. And yet he might've known she'd ignore him when Bennett said, "Tell us what?"

She turned fully toward him. "I own the bridge and the land on both sides of the river. I also built the bridge. Not Mr. Billings. Me. Mr. Hammel has been awfully careless when all he needed to do was check the deeds and tax rolls at the courthouse. It's time this was clarified. Past time. You people have been going after the wrong person."

Eyes bugged, Bennett scoffed. "The hell ya beller."

"Oh, I do beller. I do indeed."

But Shay saw the way she gazed at the ruins of her barn and frowned. It must've occurred to her that, excepting only Bent and Pinky Langley, she'd lost the most of anybody.

CHAPTER 20

Ford returned just before dawn when the sky was the color of blued skim milk. The new day had come over cloudy, the morning cool. Humidity by the creek held the pall of smoke close to the ground like fog, the smell strong and acrid.

The thud of horses' hooves brought Shay awake with a jerk. He reached for his gun as January's dog jumped from the lowboy and began barking.

He hadn't meant to close his eyes and leave January to watch the prisoners. But the wounded pair down by the bridge had gone silent, either dead, asleep, or too miserable to even moan. Bennett and the other man had nodded off in the last hour.

"It's all right," January's quiet voice stilled him before his pistol cleared the holster. "It's Ford and a couple other men." She tugged the dog's ear. "Hush, Pen," she said and the dog obeyed.

"You sure?" Shay said.

"Yes. Ford whistled a quail's call a minute ago. It's him." She shrugged. "Didn't sound much like a quail either."

"No. He never was tonally inclined." Shay shifted, trying to ease a kink out of his back, and nodded toward their prisoners. "Sorry I passed out on you. These fellers give you any trouble?"

"No." She huffed out a small laugh. "Apparently even outlaws need sleep."

Scrubbing at gritty eyes, Shay muttered, "They ain't the only ones." He'd slept for only twenty minutes, not enough by about eleven hours and forty minutes.

As he came closer, the growing light showed Ford looked the worse for wear as well, no doubt from having spent most of the last twenty-four hours aboard a horse. At least the horse was comparatively fresh, borrowed from the livery stable in town.

Two men rode beside him. Herb Schlinger, for one, his deputy badge of office restored to him by T. T. Thurston as head of the county commissioners. None other than Jess Langley, Bent's eldest son, twenty years old with his badge proudly displayed, was the other.

Ford and his companions drew rein beside the lowboy and surveyed the pair of them. "If you two aren't a sorry sight, I've never seen one. Glad to see you made it through the night. And so did the prisoners."

Shay thought he heard a little surprise. "Sure," he said. "They didn't make trouble and we ain't murderers. Not like they are. We'll wait on the law and come to their hanging."

A pained frown flitted across January's face.

"The hell," Bennett, awakened by the talk, broke in. "You won't hang me."

Ford smirked. "We'll see."

"You won't." Bennett sounded supremely sure of himself for someone with his hands tied behind him. "The boss'll be here soon. He'll bring the boys and, one way or another, have us freed up in no time. Young Eddie, he's gonna be powerful mad about missing the fun so you'd better watch out." The outlaw cocked his head toward the dead man laid out a few feet away. "Burch there was one of his friends. Eddie ain't going to take his getting killed lightly and Eddie, he's a bad one to cross. You'll see."

Shay might've been the only one who saw the flicker of movement down by the bridge. One of those men had awakened. Unless his nerves were shot and he was seeing things.

"Eddie isn't going to say anything about anything," Ford said, the corners of his mouth turning up under his mustache. "He's dead. Him and Billy Perkins both and tucked away as a surprise for Hammel."

Bennett's mouth dropped open. "Dead?"

"You heard me. Me and Billings . . ." he hesitated and in a different tone said, "seen to their bodies last night."

And that, in Shay's opinion, was one of the things about Ford he didn't care for. Ford took his pursuit of justice too far sometimes and had a little too much joy in the administration of it. Truth to tell, he'd as soon the death of Hammel's son not been announced just yet. Especially in such a loud voice with a hint of brag in it. Even Deputy Schlinger seemed surprised.

January's pretty dark eyes opened wide and she stared at him.

Unwilling to comment, Shay shook his head. Looked as though, after all the care they'd taken to arrange the bodies to appear a result of a shoot-out between outlaws, Ford had decided it no longer mattered.

Bennett seemed to think it did. A blue streak of cussing left the man almost breathless but when he could talk again, he had plenty to say. For instance, the warning that Hammel wouldn't take his boy's death lying down. That the two of them, Tervo and Billings, would both be dead by the time this day was over.

"Hell," he added, "probably before noon. Hammel ain't going to waste time being nice, I guarantee. Billings will go first. Then you, Tervo. That badge won't protect you none. Count on it."

When he quieted, January posed a safer question to Ford. "Is Dr. LeBret coming to take care of the wounded?"

She may have meant herself although Shay didn't think so.

"Yeah, he'll be along soon." Ford acted pleased to change the subject. "He's driving a wagon he's got fitted out for an ambulance. Guess it wouldn't hurt if we put everybody together in one place."

He turned to his deputies and cocked a thumb. "You boys want to fetch those two up from the bridge?"

While the deputies hurried to secure the wounded, Ford busied himself rounding up those of the outlaw's horses he could find, most of them not having strayed too far. In minutes, he had Bennett and the other unwounded outlaw mounted and ready for the trek into town. He'd found another body concealed under a bush, most probably having been shot by someone in his own gang. Another candidate for Doc's dead wagon.

They discovered an outlaw missing when the two deputies showed up toting only a single groaning man between them.

"Thought you said there was two of them," Schlinger said, puffing a little because the outlaw was big and the deputy had grown a paunch of his own large enough to steal his breath. "But this is the only man we found."

"Could be somebody fell in the crick," Jess Langley added. "Thought I saw some scraped over dirt like he might've crawled down to the water for a drink."

Ford wasn't buying it. "A drink? Doubt it. I came up short on the horses, too." He glanced over at Shay. "You know who he's going to come after, don't you?"

Shay knew what he meant.

Bennett rumbled out a hoarse laugh. "I figure there won't be nothing left of your outfit by tonight, Billings. It'll look just like this place, burnt out and all them critters you're so proud of turned into coyote bait. Hammel will see to it as quick as Jameson makes it to the dam and reports. You should've sold out when you had the chance."

Anger burned through Shay, heating the blood in his veins to boiling. Spinning away, he stalked off toward the rear of the smoldering barn, a piercing whistle splitting the morning air.

"What's he doing?" he heard Ford ask, seemingly of no one in particular. "Where's he going?"

January answered, her voice matter of fact. "He's calling Hoot. He's going to protect his home. Even if it kills him."

As good as any trained dog, Hoot came to Shay's whistle. He was fresh from having grazed the night away on January's lush pasture with his friends Ernie and Molly and even the lone cow.

A stab of pain rocked Shay's sore side as he hefted the saddle onto Hoot's back but a sense of urgency kept him from flinching. Grabbing the dangling cinch, he ran the strap through the ring and pulled it tight.

January, her eyes dark with worry, limped

266

over to him. "You shouldn't go alone, Shay. It's hard telling how many more men Hammel has working for him. You can't fight off a whole army. They'll kill you for sure."

He glanced down at her, his jaw set. "They've been trying. Haven't succccded so far. And they're not going to succeed now. Not as long as I can make it home first. Besides, we don't know that Hammel has an army. Seems to me we've cleared out a bunch of them."

"True. But we also don't know how long that man has been gone. Whether two or ten, they could be there already, waiting for you."

He looked toward the hills where his ranch lay and shook his head. "Don't see any smoke. Not yet."

Lowering the stirrup, he prepared to mount. Her hand on his stopped him.

"Ask one of those deputies to go with you. Please," she said.

A smile quirked his lips. Somehow, not saying how it happened, Hoot's gray body came between them and the others, hiding them from view.

"I'd hate to have all the hard work I put into saving your life . . ." she was saying until his lips on hers stopped all speech.

Just a little peck, he figured. Kind of goodbye and thanks. But then he got started and it turned into more. And by dog's ears, she wasn't fighting it. No, she wasn't.

Then Hoot pushed against him and it was over, except their hands were linked.

January stared at him, eyes wide. "You kissed me." It came out a whisper—but not an accusation. Her hand came up and she fingered the scar on her cheek.

Unable to help himself, he bent forward again. "You kissed me back." His voice was as low as hers.

Leave it to Ford to come riding up just then and spoil the moment. And, as Shay remembered, not for the first time in their acquaintance. There'd been that hurdy-gurdy girl over in Davenport, for instance. But this time he truly resented it until Ford said, "I'm coming with you, Billings. Time to end this ruckus before more men are killed." He spared a glance at January. "Or women."

"What about your prisoners?"

"They're tied up tighter than a drum and not going anywhere but where I say they go. Schlinger and Langley can take care of them. And Doc LeBret is coming up the road as we speak. He'll haul off the dead and wounded. I doubt Hammel is worrying about them anyhow. I figure he's coming after you."

Yeah, Shay figured so, too. He winked at January and swung aboard Hoot. "Time's a wasting," he said. "Let's go."

At the bridge he looked back. January stood watching, her expression somber.

• • •

Shay and Ford rode hard. Hoot, sensing his home pasture, pulled ahead, Ford's livery horse lacking the stamina to keep up.

At the cut-off to the ranch, Shay stopped to wait for Ford and point out a faint trail that led around back of his barn. "See that? We'll split up here. If Hammel is waiting for us—for me—he won't be expecting anyone coming from the east. You can ride up on him without being seen."

Ford didn't waste time arguing. He nodded. "Remember, Shay. Hammel don't ride anywhere alone. He's always got one or two men with him and they're paid to do whatever he says."

"I'll keep that in mind."

Hidden by the last hill, Ford urged his horse onto the path while Shay kept Hoot to a walk on the road. After allowing what he considered a sufficient amount of time for the marshal to get beyond the barn, he urged Hoot into a lope, not drawing up until they were within a hundred yards of his house.

The wrongness hit him right away.

Brin. Where was she?

His old hound should've been there to meet him.

Shay pulled his carbine from the saddle scabbard, clutching it with the stock under his elbow, ready to snap up and shoot.

At first glance, he didn't see a thing off kilter—

aside from the missing Brin and an almost eerie silence. No birds, no bugs, even the trees of his orchard where nary a leaf stirred. Otherwise, the yard looked just like it had last night when he and Ford toted those bodies away. Except for the area where he'd spread chicken manure over the bloodstains. He squinted. That appeared disturbed.

Hoot pranced a little as he came closer.

Could be Brin, bothered by the smell, had dug around in it, he supposed but he didn't think so. At this distance, it looked more like horses had tromped through the yard and stirred things up.

Several horses. Speaking of which, his prize mare and her foal stood motionless in the corral. The mare usually welcomed Hoot home with a nicker and a toss of her pretty head but not today. The mare's attention was fixed on something else.

As he came even with the house, Shay spotted a rifle barrel poked around the corner of the barn where the manure pile rose high. Whoever held the rifle fired, the report loud as it echoed off the surrounding hills. He had only an instant to fling himself off Hoot, swatting the horse on the rump as he went. The startled horse lunged ahead while Shay dropped to the ground and rolled up close to the steps, making himself small in their shadow.

In the corral, the mare and foal tore off to the

farthest corner, snorting and bucking. Hoot trotted down the road a short way and stopped.

Then it was silent again.

Shay waited motionless, gritting his teeth as the pain from his barely-healed wound ebbed. His mind raced. Where a man found one vermin, he would most likely find more. Sooner or later, these would let him know how many there were and where they were hiding. When they did, by God, he'd root them out like a nest of rats.

Ford, he remembered, had always been good at sneaking up on people. Shay neither saw nor heard a sign of him until an arm clad in gray fabric, complete with leather cuffs, waved from behind the barn. The cuffs, dyed a dark red, were distinctive. Ford had always liked fancy clothes.

The marshal's forefinger pointed up toward the barn roof, then toward the man Shay had spotted.

Shay nodded, trusting Ford had him in sight. So. Two of them. He suspected more. It didn't seem likely Hammel would climb onto the barn roof or hide beside a manure pile. His dignity wouldn't stand for it. Shay figured he'd found more comfortable concealment. But where?

A scrabbling sound reached him, the small noise coming from inside the house. Then a thud and a muffled whine.

Brin.

Shay swore under his breath. Hammel had somehow snared Brin and taken cover inside the house. The man knew Shay set a lot of store by Brin. Seemed logical he figured to use the hound against him.

Gunfire erupted out by the barn, snapping Shay's attention back to the fight. Two shots fired almost in unison. One most likely came from Ford, the other from the man by the manure pile. That one wasn't shooting at Shay this time. He'd caught sight of Ford creeping up on him and stood up to get a shot. Shay could just barely see him; saw a butt and an elbow anyway.

Lifting his rifle, Shay fired at the largest part of the target. The man howled, dropping his rifle as he clawed at his rear and stumbled backward into the open. A second later, he fell to the ground, helped along by Ford's bullet in his shoulder.

Neither Ford nor Shay dared move. Ford, because Hammel would have a shot at him. Shay, because the man on the barn roof had a clear line of sight to him. A stand-off, even if the odds had evened.

Ten minutes that felt more like twenty ticked past as the stand-off continued. In the corral, the mare and her colt resumed nibbling at the grassy enclosure. Hoot wandered over to the watering trough and took a drink. A couple of Shay's beeves walked along the fence he'd repaired not more than two weeks ago. It seemed a lifetime.

The sun rose higher in a cloudless blue sky. Sweat seeped from Shay's pores as heat and light touched on the corner where he sat. He already felt dizzy, his weakened state no match for the need of water and shade.

The stalemate couldn't stand. Hammel broke first. Ford's shadow darkened the ground as he moved and Hammel fired a few inches to the right of it.

Ford yipped, whether pinked or only startled Shay couldn't tell. Whichever, it stirred him to action. He darted from cover and before Hammel could react, snapped off a couple shots at the house, the glass in the window shattering and falling to the ground.

Shay cussed as Ford leapt back to cover before either Hammel or his remaining hired gun could bring their firearms into play. Hammel with a revolver, the man on the barn roof with a rifle.

No one was hit but Hammel, his temper getting the better of him, called out, "You, there, Bridger. Get the son of a bitch."

The sun beating down on Hammel's man on the roof may have skewed his judgement. As if he'd been waiting for the word, he scrambled over the peak and started down the other side. Looking for Ford, Shay realized. The fellow, skinny and young, appeared to have forgotten Shay.

Seemed like shooting a duck on a pond but when it came to saving Ford or shooting the man, Shay did his duty. He jerked up his rifle and let fly.

The .44 bullet smacking into the feller's chest took his legs out from under him. With a yelp of despair, he completed a slow slide off the roof, hitting the ground with a thump where he lay still. Still as death.

"Look here, Hammel," Ford yelled out. "Your men are dead. Those big plans of yours have failed. It's just you against Billings and me now. Time to give up and go quietly."

The house walls standing between them muffled Hammel's reply. "You ain't got me yet, you traitor-ass goat-eater. I oughta have guessed a man of your breeding couldn't be trusted. Foreign scum. But see, I'm not alone. I've got a brindle hound in here with me and I'm thinking she might be my ticket outta here. Isn't that right, Billings?"

Rage shook Shay. He couldn't see Hammel but he knew the man well enough to hear a nasty smirk in his words. Damn him. He read Shay right.

"Tell you what, Billings. I know you for a man of your word. Well, so am I. You let me leave and I won't shoot the dog. Deal?"

Five minutes later, Hammel walked out the door, leaving it open behind him. He carried his revolver in one hand pressed right up against Brin's head. His other was clenched in the rope encircling her neck, wound so tight Shay saw she was halfway to choking. Hammel dragged her, the hound's toenails catching on the porch boards as Brin resisted. Her eyes swiveled to follow Shay as he stood by, helpless.

Hammel stopped, his gun lifting toward Shay before a motion from Ford stopped him.

"You win for now," Ford said. "But don't push it. I ain't as committed to that dog as Billings is."

"Yeah? I wonder if you're as committed to that damn woman." His pistol back on Brin, Hammel's expression hardened. "She should've been the first one Eddie killed. Maybe the only one. Nobody would ever have missed her. She's ruined me."

"Don't you blame Miss Schutt for your troubles," Shay said. "Blame yourself and your son and your cheap-bought sheriff."

Hammel snorted his disgust. "Rhodes. Not so cheap, but a bad investment on my part. Stay back. I'll get my horse, then I'm leaving and this hound is going with me. I don't like the way you act, you know I'll shoot her."

Ignoring the part about staying back, Ford kept his rifle trained on Hammel and followed him to the barn. Brin, snapping and trying to bite, resisted best she was able.

After a brief pause, Hammel, mounted on his bay, rode out. Brin's lead was longer now but the outlaw kept the rope taut. He kicked his bay into a lope, the hound struggling to keep up.

"God dammit," Shay said. "I should've shot him where he stood."

Ford's jaw set. "He'll kill that dog anyway. You realize where he's headed, don't you? He's going after Miss January now. He'll go after her even if it means he gets caught."

"I know it," Shay said grimly. He whistled for Hoot. "But that just ain't going to happen."

Hoot, as obedient as most dogs, trotted to him. Shay swung into the saddle.

"Wait," Ford said, "I'll get my horse. It's tied to an apple tree over that rise."

But Shay wasn't waiting. He clucked to Hoot and leaned forward, urging the horse into a trot. He was five minutes behind Hammel. Five minutes more waiting for Ford could spell the difference of whether January Schutt lived or died.

CHAPTER 21

Dr. LeBret daubed carbolic over January's leg before inserting an untidy row of stitches. He hummed a tune as he worked.

January held her breath during the ordeal and tried not to scream. Confession time—his ministrations hurt more than when she received the original wound. And really! Humming? Why would one hum when unable to carry a tune? For the first time she understood why Shay had not perhaps been as welcoming to the doc's visits as he might've been. LeBret was not the most gentle of physicians, in her opinion, although his advice showed concern.

"You'd better come into town with me." He finished winding a fat bandage around the wound. Standing up, he pressed a hand to the small of his back and, apparently for the first time, observed the remains of what had been her home. "I'm sure the Ladies Aid will be delighted to put together some things to see you through. A change of clothes, maybe a spare pot, a plate and spoon."

January shook her head. She didn't care to beg for other folks' leftovers even if their intentions were good. But Doc's words served to remind her that when she escaped the fire through the hidden entrance, she'd paused to snatch up the satchel that contained most of her money and the deed to the homestead. As long as it hadn't been discovered, it must still be where she'd dropped it when Rhodes shot her. Which, as she remembered, should be far enough away from the fire to be comparatively unscathed. If safe, she had the means to buy her own change of clothes and a pot and spoon.

But not enough to start over and build a house.

"Thanks for the offer," she said. "I'll be all right. I'm going to wait here until Shay—Mr. Billings—lets me know what's happened at his ranch. I—"

Doc smirked as he climbed onto the seat of his ambulance. "Well, I know you for a lady who's not easily dissuaded from what she sets out to do. If you change your mind about the clothes, come and talk to my wife. She's a pillar of the Ladies Aid and thrives on helping folks out."

Funny. It had never occurred to her that LeBret might have a wife.

Glad to be alone at last, with Pen at her side, she watched the doctor drive away, his ambulance laden with the living lying right alongside the dead. She was relieved, and a little surprised, not to be among them. And yet the silent emptiness surrounding her as he drove out of sight didn't really feel peaceful. To the contrary.

January fell asleep curled on the lowboy's bed as she waited for Shay's return. Or at least word from him. She slept hard and heavily for an hour, then a second and a third.

Pen woke her, the dog's tail lashing against her face.

Muttering, January opened one eye. "Leave me be, Pen. I'm so awfully tired."

The dog paid no attention. The tail kept twitching, pricked ears pointed, an odd sound somewhere between a growl and a whine issuing from her throat. Stiff-legged, she stood facing the bridge and the road leading to Shay's ranch.

January suppressed a groan as she sat up. Her wound hurt like the dickens, exhaustion dogged her, and Pen's behavior could only mean one thing.

The trouble she'd sensed earlier had arrived.

And here she sat, right out in the open. Stupid. Worse, dangerous.

Pen, all her senses on high alert, had proved herself a valuable companion once again. If it hadn't been for the dog's warning, January would've been caught asleep.

Wrangling herself off the lowboy, she flopped onto her stomach behind a pile of rocks seconds before a rider appeared. She recognized the bay horse by the way it threw its head in a showy sort of way. The horse belonged to Marvin Hammel and his direction of travel indicated he'd paid a visit to Shay's ranch.

Where was Shay? Where, for that matter, was Ford?

Although the day was warm, January shivered. Dead? Both of them?

Hammel stopped at the bridge and sat there studying the scene long enough for the horse to grow impatient. Then, evidently not seeing anything to alarm him, Hammel spurred the horse and they came on.

January ducked, hugging Pen to her with an arm thrown over the dog. Go away. The words reverberated in her head so loudly that for a moment she thought she'd said them out loud.

But evidently not.

Hammel rode past her without looking her way. He circled around the barn and disappeared from her sight. Presently, she saw him riding out to the chicken coop, then on down to the river where she'd captured Rhodes.

Looking for her, she guessed.

Before she felt safe enough to move, he came back, the bay prancing under a tight rein. When he reached the area where half-burned timbers smoldered, he stopped, stared down, and dismounted.

"What's he doing?" she whispered to Pen.

The dog's muscles tensed.

But then she knew. He'd found the satchel with her money and her papers, including the deed to the property.

Teeth flashed as, grinning to himself, he tied the bag onto the back of his saddle and remounted. He must've been confident he was alone because he wasn't paying attention when she rose up and stepped in front of the bay. Not until the horse shied at the sudden appearance of a dirty, smoke-stained woman and an irate dog who felt free to bark long and loud.

The bay tossed its head, half-rearing, mane flying.

"What the . . ." Hammel snatched out the pistol holstered at his right hip. "You! What the hell does it take kill you, woman?"

Tempted to grab for her .38, she didn't. Not yet. Clamping onto the horse's chin strap, she held on tight and stood to Hammel's left. He'd have to shoot over his horse's neck to get at her. Awkward and apt to kill the horse the way this one fidgeted.

"That's my bag," she said. "I'll thank you to let it drop."

His lip curled. "Yours? Oh, I don't think so. What would a tramp like you be doing with a nice leather bag like this?" His gaze fixed on her scarred cheek.

She squinted up at him and sneered. "What would a thief like you be doing with it?"

Face flushing, he spurred the horse, making it jump ahead. January held firm even as she was lifted off her feet. Circling the horse at a safe distance, Pen kept up a continuous barking, upsetting the bay even further.

"I wanted that bridge," Hammel said. "One way or another, didn't matter how. I needed it. If I had that bridge, I'd be set." He waved the pistol at her. "But you. Between you and Billings, you've ruined me."

"You ruined yourself, Mr. Hammel. You've committed murder and arson in the name of greed. You've coerced innocent people and resorted to downright theft. Everybody in this country knows it. And now the governor and the courts know it, too."

"Murder?" Hammel caught at the ugly word. "Oh, no. I didn't kill anybody. Eddie did. It was Eddie. But now my boy is dead. He's the one murdered. Maybe you did it. He informed me what that vicious dog of yours did to his hand. And you hit him in the face. What kind of woman does a thing like that?" His lips drew back in a pseudo grin. "Well, somebody has to pay. A life for a life. I guess that means you."

Hadn't he heard a word she said? Had he completely lost his mind?

No. She didn't think so. He sounded like a man in a rage already thinking up excuses for why he committed murder. Her murder. She had experience with such a man, never to be forgotten. Her grandfather had been a man much like Hammel.

But this time she wasn't ten years old and helpless.

This time she could fight. Would fight.

Motionless, Brin lay on her side a quarter mile down the road from the turn-off to his ranch. Shay'd spotted the dark lump of her body at a distance and figured she was dead even though he hadn't heard a shot. Stepping from the saddle, he hunkered beside her. The rope still encircled her neck. He wrestled the knot loose, breaking a fingernail short enough to bleed as he hurried.

The hound proved tough. With the rope released, she drew a breath, then another. Her sides pumped in and out like a bellows. Her dry tongue poked from the side of her mouth.

"C'mon now, old girl. You'll be all right." His canteen hung from his saddle. Thoughtfully, January had filled it before he left. He just hoped they both lived long enough for him to say thanks. He poured water into his hat and held it for the dog. She lapped weakly before letting her head fall back.

Shay stroked her head and felt over her body. Except for a shallow wound where the rope had torn away the hair and burned her neck as she fought Hammel, she seemed unhurt. Lack of air and too many years had done her in. Temporarily, if her luck held. Nothing else he could do would help except let her rest.

But maybe he could do something for January.

He gave the dog a final pat and another drink before remounting Hoot. Brin would go home when she was able. If she were able.

Meanwhile, Hammel had gotten farther ahead, a worry that dug at Shay. He's the one who'd rid the world of Eddie Hammel but it looked like January might bear the brunt of his guilt. If you could call defense of your own life "guilt."

Although Ford should've caught up by now, there was no sign of him. Shay couldn't restrain himself any longer. He urged Hoot into a lope toward the bridge.

January didn't much care for the position she found herself in. Hammel persisted in spurring his horse and trying to ride her down. The horse seemed likely to go mad with fear and pain as his rider gouged him with sharp-roweled Spanish spurs. January kept bobbing and ducking, avoiding both the horse's hooves and Hammel's gun.

She felt as though their dangerous dance had been going on for hours. Her wounded leg wouldn't stand much more abuse.

"Stop this," she said, pushing against the bay's chest. "Why don't you go? Get away while you can."

If you can is what she meant but what else could she do but encourage him to run?

Not that it mattered since he ignored her words. And worse, the horse finally gave up the battle and stopped dead, leaving a portion of her exposed.

Hammel took his shot.

A sharp tug jerked January sideways. A burning pain in her scalp made her cry out.

God help me! The thought flashed through her mind as the bay, buoyed by the gun firing from above him, charged forward, knocking her aside. Why do they always go for my head?

Seconds passed, more than a few, before she understood that she was still standing. Now what? Die or draw?

As though she lived in a bad dream, January watched Hammel haul his horse around to take another pass at her. Still part of the dream, the .38 filled her hand without her being aware. And then, ever so coolly, she pointed the business end of the revolver at Hammel and squeezed the trigger.

Hammel hit the ground with a thud. His body writhed, then went still. The bay horse ran off toward the bridge.

A little dizzy, January sank to the ground and put her head on her knees. Pen, quiet now, came over and sat beside her.

"Well, Pen. I guess—" She stopped, not knowing what else to say.

Blood trickled slowly down her neck, making

her shirt collar sticky. The discomfort is what made her lift her head and when she did, she caught sight of what she first thought was a snake lying not five feet away. But the object, a medium-brown color with copper highlights, didn't move. She frowned, needing several blinks of her eyes before she recognized what lay there. Her hand reached for the back of her head.

Her hair. The long braid that had a habit of twisting and lying over her right shoulder instead of down the center of her back. Hammel had shot it plumb off, barely nicking her scalp along the way, and there it lay. On the ground. Instead of her whole body.

January laughed then. Laughed and laughed until Pen, big dog though she was, crawled onto her mistress's lap and licked her face.

She was still laughing when Shay arrived at last.

CHAPTER 22

Shay held the braided rope of January's hair, staring down and running the silken mass through his fingers as the plaiting came undone.

January wondered what he was thinking. Did he see her as a scarred killer? A destitute female in danger of becoming a clinging hanger-on, forever relying on him to provide for her? Or as an object of pity, perhaps one regarded with horror?

Anger stirred. Just because she'd never shot a man before this . . . this war started, didn't mean she wouldn't defend herself. Her property and her person. Shay must know that. And maybe she hit where she aimed because instead of being too terrified to function, she became cold and determined. Wasn't that what anyone was entitled to do?

As for providing for herself—well, she guessed she'd proved capability on that score many times over. And she'd do it again. How to begin just remained a bit of a puzzle.

The silence between them drew out.

They hadn't spoken for a long time after Shay'd gotten there and taken in the situation. Including, to January's embarrassment, the tears running down her cheeks. He seemed to think they stemmed from fear, or pain, or something.

She hadn't the nerve to tell him they were tears of laughter.

How many people, after all, had their hair shot off and lived to tell about it? Wasn't that supremely lucky and funny, too? Funny that she'd lived through the whole ordeal? Hilarious, even?

Shay didn't seem to think so. He just kept staring down and dangling the hank of her hair. Every once in a while he muttered something that sounded like "close call" or "sorry" and included a cuss word to two.

January knew they were both relieved when Ford rode up at last.

"You're late," Shay said and added grudgingly, "so was I. January has taken care of your criminal for you."

Ford urged his horse over to where Hammel's body lay sprawled and stared down. "Simplifies matters," he said in a flat voice. "Saves the state some money, too. The judge'll be glad of that."

For the first time, he seemed to notice January's shorn hair and blood-spotted attire as well as the braid Shay held in his hand. One of his eyebrows arched. "Are you hurt, Miss January?"

January reached for the back of her head, feeling the odd lightness where the weight of her hair should be. The bleeding had stopped. There hadn't really been much, considering.

"I don't think so," she said. "No."

He frowned. "Strange time to cut your hair."

She burst out laughing again.

With infinite sensitivity, Shay said, "I got a pair of scissors over at the house, Miss January. Reckon I could straighten the ends out for you. Even it up some."

"Does it look terribly bad?"

A grin flashed even though she could tell he tried to suppress it. "Kind of like somebody spun you through one of them eggbeater gadgets."

After catching Hammel's runaway horse, the men hoisted the dead man's body onto the nervous animal and were in the process of tying it down. The horse, neither of them were surprised to see, objected and they were both leery of his half-broke ways.

"He called me a traitor-ass goat-eater," Ford said, standing back and observing the position of the body belly down over the saddle.

"Who? Hammel?" Shay's grin quirked. "You ever ate goat?" He patted the horse's neck and whispered to him. Didn't seem to help much.

"Hell, no. And I don't plan on ever eating goat."

"I did once. Down in Mexico. It ain't so bad if you get a young one."

"You can have it." Ford reached under the bay's belly, avoided a kick by inches, and tied the rope dangling from Hammel's hands to his

289

feet, insuring the body stayed in place. Breathing hard, he straightened up. "What are you gonna do about Miss January?"

Shay figured his face turned red considering the sudden flush of heat and the fact he broke into a sweat. "Do? Me?"

Ford pretended to gawk around. "You see anybody else I might be asking?"

The thing is, Shay'd been considering this very question on his own accord. Pondering hard, in fact. He didn't need Ford Tervo sticking his oar into what might be deep waters. Now he thought back, Tervo always had been as curious, unless he meant as nosy, as a gossipy old woman.

"January Schutt don't need me to do anything for her. She's as independent as a hog on ice. You oughta know that as well as anyone," he said. But was that true? She'd had plans for this place, plans now destroyed. And here she was, destitute.

Ford just cocked a doubtful brow at him and cast a telling look around the place. "You sure about that?"

Well, no, he wasn't sure.

Between the two of them, except he'd better include January in the group so he guessed he meant amongst the three of them, they'd gotten this affair pretty well cleared up. In Shay's opinion, it was time Ford mounted his horse and took Hammel's body to town. Past time. Somebody would have to notify Mrs. Hammel not only about her husband but her son's demise. The sooner the better, too, so's she didn't hear it by way of some quick-spreading rumor.

Better Ford than him because he suspected Missus Hammel might've been a driving force behind Hammel's ambition if not part of the whole shady deal. Furthermore, the whole countryside knew her for an indulgent mother when it came to Edgar's wild ways. She wasn't going to take this well.

If Ford only knew, he was going to have something a whole lot more onerous to think about than what Shay Billings had to say to Miss January Schutt.

The Deputy U.S. Marshal, leading the half-wild bay and its burden, was only a speck in the distance when Shay finally got up his nerve to face January. She sat on the lowboy again, a vehicle now performing—in view of the destruction of all her other assets—as a couch, a chair, a bed and, most probably, her kitchen table and a closet for a non-existent wardrobe.

Shay cleared his throat and sat beside her. On her scarred side which, for just a moment, gave him pause. He cleared his throat again.

January looked up at him. "Got a frog?"

Reaching over, he took one of her work-worn hands in his. "No. But Miss January, I've got a working ranch. I've been thinking . . . been wondering . . . been hoping . . ." He settled on the last option. "Been hoping you might consider joining up with me."

He was lightheaded, about like he imagined a Victorian lady on the verge of fainting might feel. "Hoping you might consider marrying me." Doggedly, he continued. "I've got a house. I'd like to have someone to share it with. I'd like to share it with you."

Her fingers clenched over his so hard he thought she might paralyze them. Just once, then she tried to pull away. She stared out over her bridge. Reaching up with her free hand, she touched her scarred cheek.

She didn't say anything for the longest time and Shay had no idea what she was thinking.

"Please, Miss January," he added finally before releasing her hand. Maybe he hadn't been romantic enough—women wanted romance, didn't they?—but in his own defense, he'd never asked a woman to marry him before.

His heart was thudding to beat two of a kind and felt like to break on out of the rib cage. Oddly enough, she reached up and touched her own chest just where her heart would be. Her, too?

She drew in a deep breath and turned to face him. "Do you love me?" she asked, straight out. Her voice held a quaver.

What did she want him to say?

He held her in deep regard, revered her for

saving his life, admired her courage and for the things she'd accomplished, a woman alone. Was that love?

Her eyes met his as the silence between them deepened.

Her dog loved her. He suspected his own dog loved her. And Hoot was fine with her. What's more, she had pretty eyes. Real pretty. In fact, looking past the scar, she was altogether a fine-looking woman.

Shay smiled. Except she was dirty and sooty right now and, truthfully, a little on the stinky side. That chopped-off hair stuck out all over her head and her clothes had burn holes in them. Kind of on the disreputable side when he thought about it.

Reaching out, he tipped up her chin. "Why, yes, Miss January Schutt. I reckon I do. I love you fine," he said and set his lips against hers.

As for January? Well, seemed to him that she settled into his arms like she belonged there.

ABOUT THE AUTHOR

C. K. Crigger was born and raised in North Idaho on the Coeur d'Alene Indian Reservation, and currently lives with her husband, three feisty little dogs and an uppity Persian cat in Spokane Valley, Washington.

Imbued with an abiding love of western traditions and wide-open spaces, Crigger writes of free-spirited people who break from their standard roles.

Her short story, "Aldy Neal's Ghost," was a 2007 Spur finalist. *Black Crossing*, won the 2008 EPIC Award in the historical/western category. *Letter of the Law* was a 2009 Spur finalist in the audio category.

Center Point Large Print
600 Brooks Road / PO Box 1
Thorndike, ME 04986-0001 USA

(207) 568-3717

US & Canada:
1 800 929-9108
www.centerpointlargeprint.com